THE PUMPKINS OF TIME

by

MEL GILDEN

BROWNDEER PRESS

HARCOURT BRACE & COMPANY

New York   San Diego   London

Requests for permission to make copies of any part of the
work should be mailed to: Permissions Department,
Harcourt Brace & Company, 6277 Sea Harbor Drive,
Orlando, Florida 32887-6777.

Browndeer Press is a registered trademark of
Harcourt Brace & Company.

Library of Congress Cataloging-in-Publication Data
Gilden, Mel.
The pumpkins of time/by Mel Gilden.
p.   cm.
"Browndeer Press."
Summary: Fourteen–year–old Myron finds that he has
become very interesting to a menacing alien from outer space.
ISBN 0-15-276603-0 (hc).—ISBN 0-15-200889-6 (pbk.)
[1. Science fiction.   2. Extraterrestrial beings—Fiction.]
I. Title.
PZ7.G386Pu   1994
[Fic]—dc20   94-16894

The text was set in Janson.

Designed by Lori J. McThomas
Printed in Hong Kong
First edition
A B C D E

For Linda Zuckerman,
who is as weird as anybody
but dresses nicer

CONTENTS

TIME LEAP I

NO ONE IS WAITING IN THE DARKNESS OUT BEYOND PLUTO WHEN THE VEHICLE PASSES.

BUT IF SOMEBODY WERE THERE AND COULD WITHSTAND THE LACK OF HEAT AND PRESSURE AND AIR, THE VIEWER WOULD SEE A STREAK COMING IN FAST FROM THE DEPTHS OF INTERSTELLAR SPACE.

AS THE VEHICLE MAKING THE STREAK PASSES, THE VIEWER WOULD SEE THAT IT IS NOT A SHIP OR A COMET OR A WEIRD ALIEN. A QUICK-EYED EARTHPERSON COULD IDENTIFY THE VEHICLE AS AN ANCIENT INTERNATIONAL HARVESTER PICKUP TRUCK.

OF COURSE, ANY VIEWER WOULD HAVE TO LOOK SHARP BECAUSE IT GOES BY AT MANY TIMES THE SPEED OF LIGHT.

THE PICKUP TRUCK DIVES DOWN THE SUN'S GRAVITY WELL, DOWN TO WHERE THE INHABITED PLANETS TOAST THEIR TOES AT THE SUN'S HEARTH.

IT ORBITS THE SUN ONCE LIKE A DOG SNIFFING FOR A PARTICULAR SCENT AND THEN SHOOTS TOWARD A PLANET THAT MANY OF ITS INHABITANTS CALL EARTH.

1 CRAZY FOR SUPERHEROES

As he rode on the bus that would take him across town, Myron Duberville could not help feeling guilty. Not because he should be helping with his uncle Hugo's time experiments—Princess would be there, after all. And his new interest wasn't illegal, immoral, or fattening. Yet Myron was certain that it was wrong, especially for a kid who wanted to be an accountant when he grew up.

OK, so he was some kind of pervert. As long as Princess and Uncle Hugo didn't find out, he would be all right. If they did find out, they'd probably never stop kidding him. Which was a heck of a situation because it was their fault he had this hobby, anyway. He'd only become interested in this strange stuff after he and Princess and Uncle Hugo had sent aliens home in a 1960 Chevrolet Belvedere. Something in his mind had snapped and he began collecting comics.

Being a little goofy wasn't so bad, really. He could see now that he'd been a snob before—a little stiff, and not much fun. As he looked disapprovingly out the grimy window, he realized he hadn't abandoned his old ways entirely. Dirt was still the constant enemy, and he still regarded his uncle as lovable but crazy.

As far as Princess was concerned—what could he say? They were about the same age, but she was larger, the kind of girl Myron's mom called big-boned. She wore her dark hair in bangs that nearly touched the top of her glasses. Though she was just a girl, Princess had proven to be steadfast and useful in the alien crisis. Myron had even begun to think of her as his friend, a turn of events that disturbed him in ways he could not explain or describe, not even to himself. Also, Princess was a natty dresser, as Myron was. But while he dressed nicely because he liked to feel neat and clean, he suspected that Princess just liked to look good.

He got off at his stop and once again checked a sheet of paper for the address. He walked up the block of nice houses, so excited he could barely contain himself. "Biff, bam, zowie!" he muttered happily.

Ahead of him a couple of little kids were playing catch with a basketball. One of the kids threw wildly, and the ball flew out into the street.

Imagining a yellow cape rippling behind him, Myron leaped forward. "You kids wait here!" he called.

They looked at him with wide, amazed eyes but waited as he retrieved their ball. He gave it back to the kid who had thrown it. "Be more careful next time," Myron cautioned them. "And remember to eat right, get plenty of rest, and brush your teeth regularly."

"Yes, sir," the kid said, though he seemed a little confused. Myron chuckled. How could mere mortals understand the deeds of superheroes?

The house he'd been searching for looked similar to many of the others he'd passed. The woman who answered the door blinked at him. She was tall and thin, and wore an apron with flowers on it. Her hair was short and white.

"Mrs. Trubole?" Myron asked.

"You must be Myron," the woman said pleasantly enough. "Come on upstairs."

She led him to her son's room. On the walls hung posters of baseball players, rock musicians, and the starship *Enterprise*. Rows of plastic model airplanes were lined up on his dresser. Apparently, Brandon Trubole was into more than comic books.

Mrs. Trubole stood stiffly at the door. "I thought that while Brandon was away at college I would clean up his room a little, get rid of some of the junk he's been collecting since he was a kid."

"Yes, ma'am," Myron said. She'd told him all this before, on the phone. He knew that Mrs. Trubole's idea of junk included the *Spartan* comic books strewn across Brandon's bed.

"There they are," Mrs. Trubole said.

Myron sat down on the edge of the bed and began to shuffle through the *Spartan*s. The books were in good condition. Mrs. Trubole had admitted that a few issues might be missing. That was no big deal. Part of the fun was filling in holes in your collection.

Myron had refused to be bothered that some woman was selling her son's comic collection out from under him without his permission or knowledge. But sitting on the edge of Brandon's bed, the bed of a guy he didn't even know, Myron had second thoughts. How would he feel if Uncle Hugo sold off *his* collection while he was out? Of course, Hugo was not the type to do such a thing, but still, how would Myron feel? Crummy, that's how.

Myron fought with himself for a while, but at last his desire to own a nearly complete run of *The Spartan* overwhelmed his guilt at blindsiding a fellow collector. The Spartan was Myron's favorite superhero. Besides, he rationalized, if Mrs. Trubole didn't sell the *Spartan*s to him, she'd sell them to somebody else.

Myron laid out the twenty bucks he and Mrs. Trubole had agreed upon, and then loaded the comics into the paper shopping bag he'd brought along. Mrs. Trubole escorted him downstairs and gently closed the door behind him. The whole process seemed so final, Myron almost knocked on the door and gave the comics back to her.

But even while he thought about the wild and angry scene that would take place when Brandon returned from college, Myron hefted the shopping bag full of comic books and walked back to the bus. The heady odor of pulp paper rose from the bag, making Myron smile and hum.

"Biff! Bam! Zowie!" he mumbled.

The two little kids were still playing ball, but they stopped and looked at him.

"Eat your greens," Myron advised as he passed.

Myron felt very satisfied with himself as he carried the bag full of comics up the gravel driveway to Uncle Hugo's mansion, but he knew that getting into the house without being seen would be a problem. Questions would be asked. He had answers ready, and as long as somebody—Princess, for instance—didn't actually look into the bag, he'd be all right.

He let himself into the quiet mansion. A stained-glass window of Robby the Robot let in light at the far end of the foyer. Hanging from the ceiling on wires were scale models of spaceships from films and books, along with models of real spacecraft like the space shuttle and the lunar lander. Paintings of aliens and monsters were displayed on the walls.

Myron paid little attention to Uncle Hugo's strange decor; after long familiarity, he'd not only become accustomed to it, he'd actually grown to like it. This was another secret he kept from Uncle Hugo and Princess. Being a kid accountant was tough.

When Myron had first visited Uncle Hugo's mansion at the beginning of summer, he'd been surprised and a little disconcerted by the personal touches Uncle Hugo had given the place. After all, Uncle Hugo was chairman of the board of Astronetics, a major aerospace firm. As a matter of fact, Myron's dad and Hugo had started the company before Myron was born. Myron's mom was a major stockholder.

As it turned out, Hugo was preoccupied with concepts that Myron had considered no better than science fiction. Myron sensed his uncle had been disappointed that Myron seemed to lack an adventurous and open-minded spirit. He had been correct when Myron first arrived, but over the summer Myron had developed spirit to spare—which horrified and pleased him all at once.

Of course, since the business with the aliens and the Chevrolet, Myron and Hugo and Princess functioned as a team—more or less. Difficult to believe, but there it was. Frankly, he didn't know what was happening to him.

Myron was congratulating himself on getting halfway across the foyer when Uncle Hugo burst out of the library. Hugo was a handsome middle-aged guy who generally wore a lumberjack shirt and jeans—not exactly the uniform of the high-powered executive. This had distressed Myron too—back when he insisted each article of his clothing sport a fashionable little pelican. He had actually loosened up to the point where some of his clothing did not have any animal at all sewn on it.

At the moment, Uncle Hugo seemed very excited. "Myron!" he cried. "Good! You're back! I need your help!" Hugo grabbed him by the arm and pulled him into the library, forcing Myron to leave behind the shopping bag.

Every flat surface in the library was covered by pieces of ancient clay pots, stone arrowheads, peculiar rocks, and other items that had built up what Hugo called "a large temporal differential." According to the argument Hugo had made at the dinner table some weeks before, the older a thing was, the more of a temporal differential it had. Though Myron found this a difficult concept to understand or even believe, he didn't argue. After all, Hugo had been right when he maintained that some bits of junk were really space aliens.

Princess stood in front of Hugo's desk with one foot on a huge skull, as if she were posing for a photograph.

"Schmoozosaurus skull," Uncle Hugo explained. "The schmoozosaurus was apparently the most social of all dinosaurs. Their remains are never found in groups of fewer than three. The natural history museum loaned me this one for my experiments, but Princess and I can't lift it onto the desk."

Myron walked over to the skull. "No prob," he assured them. "Gravity is our friend."

They positioned themselves around the schmoozosaurus skull and on the count of three lifted it into something that looked like a huge empty fish tank. Hugo put a metal lid on top of the tank. A cable led from a knob on the lid to a confusion of wires and transistors and stuff, and from there to a big ceramic jar in which Hugo said he was going to store the time.

"What will you do with the time?" Myron had asked when Hugo first explained the setup.

"Oh, everybody needs more time," Uncle Hugo had said vaguely. "But so far what we're doing here is pure science. We're learning facts about the universe without worrying what they're good for."

Now Uncle Hugo flicked a switch, and the

mechanism began to buzz like an angry insect. "That's it," he said. "We just have to let the time drain."

"Are you sure?" Myron asked.

"If I was sure," Uncle Hugo said, "I wouldn't have to do the experiment."

"Makes sense," Princess said, and Myron could only agree.

When Uncle Hugo began sorting through his junk, Myron walked quickly from the library, hoping to get his bag upstairs before anybody noticed it.

Princess followed him out of the room. "I just found out that Ten Big Cookies is going to be at Le Place tonight," she said. "Do you want to go?"

Ten Big Cookies was the rock group she favored at the moment, and Le Place was a local teen hangout.

"The last time we went there," Myron reminded her, "I sat on a puddle of soda pop and I had to walk around sticky for the rest of the evening." He really hated to be sticky or dirty or messy, and he generally dressed more neatly than other guys who were four-teen. Rather than jeans and a T-shirt, his knocking around outfit consisted of slacks and a nice sport shirt with a pelican on the pocket. (Since coming to Uncle Hugo's mansion, he hadn't actually purchased anything with a pelican on it, but he hadn't thrown away any of his old stuff either.) Myron noticed that he continued to dress this way despite his recent interest in comic books. Maybe there was hope for him after all.

Princess shook her head. "It's a dirty world, Myron," she explained. "Get used to things like that happening occasionally, or go live in a plastic bubble."

"Dirt may be unavoidable," Myron said, "but I don't have to like it."

"Does that mean you want to go?" she asked. Her eyes struck something behind him.

"What?" Myron asked, afraid of what she'd seen.

"What's in the bag?"

"It wouldn't interest you," Myron said.

"It's a complete mint set of *The Wonderful World of Accounting*—all seven volumes."

"Wow," Princess said without enthusiasm.

"I told you," he said, hoping the conversation would just die. He grabbed the bag and mounted the stairs.

"Let me help," Princess said and reached for the bag. "I guess I can carry a few volumes."

"That's all right. I wouldn't want you to contaminate yourself."

But Princess was determined, and Myron could see no way to dissuade her without being incredibly rude and therefore raising suspicion.

They were about halfway to the second floor when a roaring began, and the whole mansion shook so hard that the joints in the walls squeaked.

The spaceships hanging from the ceiling swayed gently. Though Myron and Princess both stood calmly waiting for the noise and the shaking to pass, the vibration caused the shopping bag to tear all down one side. Myron watched with alarm as the contents spilled down the stairs in a long drift.

Soon the shaking went away, like a storm passing.

"What's this?" Princess cried with glee as she reached down and picked up a handful of comic books.

2 DANDELION WHINE

Myron postponed the inevitable confrontation for a moment more by ignoring her and going to answer the door. Uncle Hugo had rigged his front doorbell to sound like a spaceship taking off, which was what all the commotion had been about. Myron opened the door, but saw no one till he heard a small meow and looked down.

Sitting on the doormat licking a front paw

was a thin calico cat with enormous eyes. She meowed again and walked into the mansion as if she owned the joint.

"Hey look," said Myron, hoping to distract Princess from the comic books. "A cat."

Princess dropped a comic book and ran down the stairs, causing the cat to shy. "Isn't it perfect?" Princess cried. She and Myron knelt to pet the cat as it sniffed around.

"Who does it belong to?" Princess asked.

"You know as much as I do. She just walked in the door."

"Why do you call it *she?*"

"Like ninety-nine percent of calico cats are girls. It's genetic."

"You seem to be the big favorite," Princess commented as the cat purred loudly and rubbed up against Myron. "What am I, chopped liver?"

Myron petted the cat happily—he'd always liked cats—though he also didn't understand the attraction.

"If you were chopped liver," Myron said, "*you'd* probably be the big favorite."

The cat trotted up the stairs, sniffed at Myron's comic books, and sneezed. Great, Myron thought. Everybody's a critic.

"What should we call her?" Myron asked, hoping to delay the inevitable discussion about comics for as long as possible.

Princess followed the cat back up to where she'd been sitting. "This isn't *The Wonderful World of Accounting*," she said and pointed to the evidence. The cat sat down on the evidence and started to wash her paw again.

Myron sighed. "It's the illustrated version," he insisted without much hope. "It's for kids."

"Right," Princess said as she gently pulled a comic out from under the cat. "This looks like a complete run of *The Spartan*."

"I thought you only read science-fiction *books*," Myron said, "with your little finger raised and your nose in the air." He raised his little finger as if he were drinking tea from a fragile cup and lifted his nose high.

"Hey," said Princess, "I'll read anything that'll expand my mind." She sat down on the steps and flipped pages. "This is great," she said. "I didn't know you were into comics, Myron."

She sounded more enthusiastic than sarcastic, he noted with relief. "I wanted it to be a surprise," he said, knowing how lame that sounded.

"Huh?" she asked. "Why? It's nice to see you taking an interest in something important for a change."

"Accounting is important."

"Nothing is as important as expanding your mind."

"That's no problem around here," Myron commented. He sat down on a step and began to admire the garish colors on the cover of *The Spartan*, *No. 3*: "The Spartan Battles the Horrible Dr. Westinghouse—HE TURNS WATER INTO ICE!" The cat curled up against Myron and began to take long swipes at her side with her tongue.

Why had the cat picked him? Why this house? In Uncle Hugo's neighborhood, nearly all the houses were mansions, and they were all a mile or two apart. If this cat was lost, she was *really* lost. He wondered if she was hungry.

Hugo ran into the foyer. "Myron, Princess," he cried excitedly. "Come into the library! I have something to show you." Then he saw the cat and smiled. "What's this?" he asked.

"A cat," Myron said. "She just walked in and made herself at home."

"Does she have a name?"

"Not yet," Princess said.

"Great. We'll call her H.G. Wells. Now that that's settled, follow me."

"But H.G. Wells is a guy's name," Princess said. "This is a female cat."

"She seems to like it," Myron pointed out. The first time Uncle Hugo had mentioned the name, the cat stood up and pricked her ears in his direction. "You want to be H.G. Wells?" Myron asked as he scratched her between the ears.

"Meow," the cat said.

"Well, there, you see!" Uncle Hugo said. He ran into the library, and Myron and Princess could do nothing but follow. The library seemed just as they had left it. Uncle Hugo was standing with his back to them looking at something on his desk.

"What's wrong?" Myron asked.

"Come look."

Myron and Princess stepped forward and stood on either side of him. "Wow," they said together.

The schmoozosaurus skull was glowing gently, and the jar that supposedly was collecting time flickered in and out of existence like a bad fluorescent tube. In the center of the desk sat a machine about the size of a shoebox. It looked like a polished brass sleigh but with additions and modifications. Attached to the back was a big vertical disk made out of brass. On the front was a cylindrical control panel covered in black leather, with a lever and three lights. In the center of it all was a wooden chair padded with red velvet. On the chair rested a bunch of dandelions. The machine flickered in exact cadence with the jar.

It was awesome. Apparently H.G. Wells

agreed, because she leaped onto the desk and sniffed at the contrivance as if it were made of tuna.

"Way cool," said Princess. "It's H.G. Wells's time machine."

Myron had recently read the English Major's Choice comics version of *The Time Machine* by H.G. Wells (the writer, not the cat), and he knew that Princess was right.

"Yes," Uncle Hugo whispered as he stared at it.

The machine was delicately made, and parts of it did not seem real. Those, Myron knew, were the parts that extended into the fourth dimension—into time. The flickering slowed, and the glow faded. Soon everything seemed stable again. H.G. lost interest, climbed carefully into Uncle Hugo's chair, and went to sleep with her tail over her nose.

"Where did it come from?" Myron asked.

"I don't know," Hugo said. "It just appeared. Didn't you hear its arrival? The whole place shook."

"I thought it was the front doorbell," Myron said.

"So did I for a moment," Hugo said. He squatted and looked across his desk into the mechanism.

"Funny how the cat and the time machine arrived at about the same moment," Princess said.

"Funny, yes," Uncle Hugo said. "Strange. Exciting!"

"But does it mean anything?" Myron asked.

"Not yet," Uncle Hugo said, and chuckled. He shook his finger at the time machine. "Time currents caused by my experiments must have swept it to the here-and-now."

"But from where?" Princess asked.

"From the there-and-then?" said Myron.

Hugo shrugged. "Who knows? But I'll tell you this: that machine must be old because it was made to be beautiful as well as useful. These days, scientific apparatus is just made to be functional."

"It looks Victorian," Myron stated, thinking of the English Major's Choice comic book.

"What do you know about Victorian design?" Princess asked with surprise.

Myron smiled and rolled his eyes. "I had a class in it once," he said.

Princess laughed. "You're probably right," she said. "It looks a lot like the machine in the movie."

"I don't remember any dandelions in the EMC comics version, though," Myron said. He was still trying to keep his comic book collection separate from his real life, but he could see that Uncle Hugo's project and the arrival of the time machine (and the cat, too—who knew?) would make this increasingly difficult.

"Not in the movie or the book, either," Princess agreed.

"No," Uncle Hugo said. "But I'm sure they're important. I've seen dandelions like these before, growing in the ceramic jars in which I store my time."

"How can you tell?" Myron asked. "Don't all dandelions look pretty much alike?"

Hugo picked up the dandelions and studied them closely. "These are not just alike, they are all exactly the same—as if they came from the same mold." He handed them to Myron and went to the other side of his desk where he pulled open the drawer.

Princess looked over Myron's shoulder while he considered the flowers. He found a petal that was slightly smaller than the others and lined it up with a similar petal on another dandelion. While the flower was obviously real, the sizes of the petals and the way they were bent were *exactly the same* all the way around.

"I'll bet they were genetically engineered," Princess suggested.

"In the nineteenth century?" Myron asked skeptically.

Hugo shrugged. "If they could build time machines, why couldn't they do genetic engineering? You'd be surprised what can be done with rivets if they're small enough." He showed them the dandelions he'd taken from his desk drawer. They looked fresh. "You know how dandelions begin to wilt almost immediately after you pick them?"

Myron and Princess nodded.

"Well, these are almost a week old. And look . . ." He held up one of his desk flowers next to one that had arrived with the time machine. They were exactly the same.

"It must mean something," Myron said.

"Yes," Uncle Hugo said. "I believe that these flowers will improve my process."

"You mean they'll allow you to drain more time out of old things?" Princess asked.

"Not exactly," Hugo said hesitantly. "I'm afraid I have a confession to make. Draining time to be stored for later use was never my goal but only a step along the way. My goal was always to find a better way to preserve food."

Preserve food? Such a project didn't seem up to Hugo's usual standards for weirdness. Preserving food actually sounded like something a normal person would want to do. And coming right on the heels of draining the time from a schmoozosaurus skull, the arrival of the cat, and the even more mysterious arrival of a time machine loaded with identical dandelions, Uncle Hugo's interest in something so conventional was surprising as well as disappointing.

Princess frowned.

"I get it," Myron said. "You want to improve two of the four basic food groups—frozen and canned."

"What are the other two?" Uncle Hugo asked.

"Fast and spoiled," Princess said. "It's an old joke."

"This is no laughing matter," Uncle Hugo insisted. "Think about it, Myron. What makes food spoil? What makes ice cream melt? What makes pizza cool?"

"Time?" Princess suggested before Myron had a chance to respond.

"Exactly," Uncle Hugo said. "Think of the environmental impact of the perfect food keeper!"

"I'm thinking about it," Myron said. "But, well, hasn't the vacuum jug already been invented?"

Uncle Hugo waved away vacuum jugs with a look of disgust on his handsome face. "I'm not talking about chicken soup and coffee, my boy. I'm talking about solid food for the millions. Think of it." He put an arm around Myron's shoulder and, gesturing expansively with his other hand, showed Myron the future. "Vacuum jugs are not perfect keepers. A little of the outside temperature leaks in with a little of the outside air. A little of the internal conditions leaks out. Food in vacuum jugs is spoiling even as we speak! Everything goes bad eventually. Besides, a vacuum jug big enough to hold a hamburger and fries and a mocha shake is an expensive proposition. Not to mention the fact that no vacuum jug ever built could keep some things hot and some things cold *at the same time.* With my method, nothing would go bad simply because it would not get older."

"It's the Fountain of Youth," Princess

cried. "I'm sure my parents would be interested."

"I don't know," Myron said. "If something doesn't get any older, it's also not changing. Does that mean a person kept alive using Uncle Hugo's method would be a statue?"

"Suspended animation?" Princess asked.

"Maybe. Possibly. Nobody knows. See the potential?"

"That's great, sir," Princess said, "but how will these dandelions help?"

"First things first," Hugo said. He set down the dandelions on the desk. "We must discharge a responsibility to Mr. Wells, the man who built this time machine." He rested his hands on either side of the time machine and stared at it. "We can do this experiment only once," he said. "When that machine is gone, I don't believe we can ever bring it back. But that's no reason to stop its journey. Mr. Wells may be depending on it."

He scribbled something on a notepad, tore off the top sheet, and handed it to Princess. She read what he'd written, nodded, and handed the paper to Myron. The note read: "DEAR MR. WELLS: GREAT BOOK! HIP HIP HUR-RAH!" Hugo had signed their names and the date.

"That seems to cover it," Myron agreed.

He handed the paper back to Uncle Hugo, who folded it once and set it on the little red velvet chair. Uncle Hugo reached into the machine with one finger and pushed the control lever forward. They heard a distinct click, but nothing happened.

"Great," Princess said. "We broke it."

"I don't think so," Uncle Hugo said. "Perhaps these dandelions are even more important than I thought. We must assume Mr. Wells had his reasons for keeping their importance a secret—perhaps as a security measure."

Myron understood immediately. You couldn't have just anybody knocking around in time. In the comics, that sort of jaunt always led to trouble.

Uncle Hugo set the bunch of dandelions back in the chair, and covered it with the note; together they looked like a little blond man who'd fallen asleep under his newspaper. "Now," he said, as he rubbed his hands together. He reached in again with his finger. He stopped suddenly and smiled. "Perhaps you'd lend me your finger, Myron," he suggested.

Before Myron could object, Uncle Hugo grabbed his wrist. Myron pointed a finger, and with it Hugo pushed the control lever forward. They both jumped back when the big disk began to turn.

As the disk spun faster and started to whine, the room shook as if somebody were ringing the doorbell again. H.G. woke up and looked over the edge of the desk at the machine. She climbed onto the desk and sat down sphinxlike; through narrow eyes she watched with the rest of them while the machine swiveled around once, grew indistinct, and with a rising whistle disappeared entirely. It left behind only the smell of ozone and an orange glow that quickly faded.

"Wow," Princess said.

Myron could only agree with her. Apparently, dandelions were the secret ingredient, just as Uncle Hugo had guessed.

Uncle Hugo seemed very excited. "I'll be back," he cried as he ran from the room.

"Where are you going?" Myron asked.

Uncle Hugo yelled over his shoulder. "I'm going to harvest the dandelions that are growing in my time jars." He waved his sample in the air and laughed. "Just think! I've been throwing them away!" He pushed through the swinging door into the kitchen.

"Uncle Hugo's gone sane," Myron said.

"True. Wanting to preserve food seems pretty normal, but you have to admit that his chosen method—draining time from dinosaur skulls and then manipulating it with dandelions—is definitely worthy of him."

"Maybe," Myron said. "Either way, the whole project doesn't interest me much. Uncle Hugo has actually achieved the impossible. He's succeeded in making time travel boring." He picked up H.G., stroked her a time or two, and set her back on the desk. She sniffed at the spot where the time machine had disappeared.

"This cat is going to need some food and a litter box," Princess said.

"What about her previous owner?"

"If any. We can watch for posted notices, but until then, I'd say that she's your responsibility."

"Mine?" Myron had never owned a live thing before, and the prospect seemed daunting.

"You're the one she likes. See?"

H.G. had jumped down and was rubbing up against his legs again.

"Come on," Princess said, "I'll help you look around the kitchen."

They had no cat food, of course, but they did find some canned chicken, which H.G. seemed to like.

"I don't know what to do about a litter box," Myron said while they watched H.G. chomp on the chicken. "Maybe she can do what she needs to do outside."

"As your uncle Hugo said, 'If we knew the

answer, we wouldn't have to do the experiment.' "

"I'm willing if the cat is." He remembered his new *Spartans* were still on the main staircase. "But I'm not going to stand around waiting for her to need a bathroom. I'm going to sort my comics," he said.

"Can I help?" Princess asked.

"You have to be careful," Myron said. "I don't want you bending covers or tearing anything. These comics are for the ages."

Princess laughed. "You don't have a thing to worry about, Myron. You're still an accountant at heart."

"You can laugh all you want, Princess, as long as you're careful. And you have to wash your hands." He walked back to the foyer, and H.G. Wells trotted after him.

3 TIME MUSH

They didn't see much of Uncle Hugo for the next few days, but that was all right because his absence gave Myron the opportunity to spend a lot of time in his room sorting his comic books.

Myron's bedroom was paneled in white plastic, and except for two chairs, a desk, and a table, it seemed featureless. Uncle Hugo had built the room to be an exact replica of the captain's cabin in the fantastically successful science-fiction movie *Skyjacks of the Universe*. Myron could make furniture and closets and futuristic equipment come and go just by pushing a button, turning a knob, or waving a hand.

He spun the closet open and pulled out pile after pile of comics. He'd been buying them for weeks—using the allowance his mom sent him—and so he had quite a collection socked away. Princess was obviously impressed. Most of Myron's comic books were of the superhero variety, but he had a few funny animal comics by famous gag writer Jack Enyart. Organizing them was a big job. His recent acquisition of *Spartan* books didn't make the job any smaller.

He planned to sort them alphabetically by series title, and then by issue number. Princess helped him, which turned out to be more fun than he'd expected once they understood each other. The problem was that Princess was pretty rough with the product and he had to constantly caution her to be more careful. H.G. helped too by sitting in the center of greatest activity. In any case, the work went slowly because they both found themselves stopping to read when they should have been sorting.

They were sitting side by side on the floor with their backs against his bed. H.G. was lounging on the stack of comics Myron had been sorting before he stopped to admire a particularly lurid cover on a *Spartan* comic that Princess was reading. On it, a man dressed like a guy in a Hercules movie knelt in pain before a big guy dressed like a Roman soldier. The guy who was kneeling was the Spartan. He was enclosed in blue fire shooting from the tip of the big Roman guy's spear.

It looked like curtains for the Spartan, but Myron knew without even opening the book that the Spartan would escape unharmed. He'd been escaping regularly for decades. Myron had discovered long ago the question wasn't *whether* the Spartan would escape but *how*.

"Don't open the book so far," Myron

reminded her for the hundredth time. "I don't want any cracks in the cover."

"You're one sick puppy," Princess said.

"Because I want my collection in good condition?" Myron asked, exasperated.

"Because you can't do anything without counting it, organizing it, and filing it away."

"I suppose your books at home are all piled in a corner like so much dirty laundry."

"Well, no," Princess admitted.

"Anyway," Myron said, "I guess that in the long run it doesn't really matter how careful I am. The acid in the comic-book paper makes the books turn brown, and eventually all you have is a pile of dust."

Myron reached to move H.G. Wells from a pile of comics to the floor, when he had a thought that stopped him. "Maybe we could get Uncle Hugo to inject time into my comic books."

"Why not?" Princess said. "If he can preserve food, comics should be a piece of cake, so to speak."

Myron enjoyed thinking about the possibilities for a moment. "Big *if*, huh?"

"Your uncle's a pretty clever guy," Princess said. "He must be doing *something* out in that barn."

The barn was an old ramshackle building, sadly in need of paint, that stood at one edge of a wild field on Uncle Hugo's estate. Hugo had electrified it and added a small modern bathroom. Out behind it were what seemed to be several acres of ceramic time jars.

Myron agreed that his uncle Hugo must be doing something out there. All yesterday afternoon, Astronetics trucks had unloaded big crates—Uncle Hugo could probably get whatever-it-was wholesale. He and Princess had gone out a few times to look around, but Hugo wouldn't let them inside.

When they got all the *Spartan*s organized, Myron could see that Mrs. Trubole had been right when she admitted the run wasn't complete. *No. 4* and *No. 7* were missing.

Myron waved his hand over the lamp on his desk, and a drawer turned out from the wall on a pivot. He rummaged in it till he found a catalog he'd sent away for. Anything he wanted he could purchase through the mail: issues of his favorite comics, polyethylene bags, storage boxes, posters of superheroes, and comic book repair kits were only the beginning. Sure enough, *The Spartan No. 4* and *No. 7* were available, but for prices that made Myron swallow hard.

Princess looked at the price list over Myron's shoulder. "Save your pennies," she advised.

"Hah," Myron said. "By the time I save that many pennies, we'll *all* be piles of dust."

Myron was still longing after items in the catalog when Hugo ran into the bedroom.

"Come on, kids," he cried, out of breath. "I want to share my findings with you."

"You have findings already?" Myron asked.

"I'm not just lounging around out there eating bonbons," Hugo replied. "Come on!"

Myron threw the catalog into the box with his comics and followed Uncle Hugo out.

"It's exciting to be Hugo's assistant," Princess said as she came up even with him. "We're always on call."

"Yeah," Myron said as he smiled. "Maybe we should invest in a beeper."

Princess laughed.

Myron was pleased to be out in the warm sunny day after sitting for so many hours in his room. They passed the disused tennis courts and followed a brick path to a gravel driveway.

At the end of it, next to the weathered barn, was an enormous heap of junk—a mountain of junk, a souvenir from Hugo's previous mania.

For the first time in days, the barn's doors were open wide. Inside were a vat and a table and a lot of laboratory equipment. In the vat was some terrible gray stuff that looked like oatmeal and gave off steam with the intensely green smell of cooked spinach. Dandelion clippings were everywhere.

Some of the equipment was digital and seemed to exist only so that lights would have a place to blink, but most of the equipment Hugo used looked as if it came from a Frankenstein movie. Banks of knifeblade switches lined one wall. Near them were tubes the size of telephone booths, each with colored water bubbling inside. One machine seemed to do nothing but go *humph-a humph-a* and puff purple smoke rings at the ceiling. All the equipment bore the Astronetics label, of course. Myron was surprised to see that they built the Frankenstein stuff, too.

Hugo strolled around the barn aiming something that looked like a TV remote at the equipment or at the stuff in the vat; he wrote down each reading in a small notebook that he kept in his shirt pocket.

"What's in here?" Myron asked with distaste as he pointed to the vat.

"It's time mush," Hugo said. "I boiled it down from the heads of the dandelions I skimmed off the bottoms of my time jars."

"What are you going to do with it?" Princess asked. She sniffed it and made a face.

"I'm going to make temporal insulation," Uncle Hugo said. The idea seemed to please him enormously.

"Temporal insulation?" Myron asked.

"You're going to make something that will keep time *out?*"

"In or out, I'm not sure which," Uncle Hugo said. "But I'm going to make cardboard with this mush, and out of the cardboard I'm going to make boxes in which it will be possible to store food forever."

"You can do that?" Princess asked.

"Using the dandelions, yes. I've discovered they warp time somehow."

"Way cool!" Myron exclaimed. "Then the dandelions really are important. How do you know they warp time?"

"See that cup of coffee?" Uncle Hugo asked as he pointed to a wooden chair on which a steaming mug of coffee sat in a large nest of dandelions. "It hasn't cooled off after three days. And over there," he pointed again, "is a box of Eskimo Tacos, the quiescently frozen treat. It's still solid after almost that long."

Myron had to admit Uncle Hugo's accomplishments were impressive. And the possibilities excited him. If the dandelions worked on coffee and ice cream, they certainly would work on comic books. He'd have to ask for one of those cardboard boxes when they were ready.

"What happens when the dandelions wilt?" Myron asked.

"They don't wilt," Hugo said. "At least, none have so far."

"Wait a minute," Princess said. "If they don't wilt, how come the world isn't hip deep in dandelions by now?"

"Don't get rambunctious, Princess," Hugo said with irritation. Then he shook his head. "But it's a good question. Maybe they just wash away along the time stream when nobody's looking."

"What does that mean?" Myron tried to get a grip on the concept.

"If I knew," Uncle Hugo said, "I'd be a lot further along in my research than I am now."

Myron was glad that he wasn't the only one who was confused.

The next thing he knew, Hugo had him stirring the noxious mixture in the big vat with a long paddle while Princess tore the heads off dandelions.

"Just remember not to add those dandelion heads too quickly," Uncle Hugo cautioned. "The time differential will become too great and we'll have quite an explosion here." For a moment, he stared at the bubbling sludge as if hypnotized, then he went out to harvest more dandelions.

The hot, sweaty work went on all afternoon while Uncle Hugo collected more flowers. As Myron stirred, Princess filled a battered saucepan with dandelion heads, and when it was full, dumped the contents into a hopper above Myron's vat. Occasionally, Myron released a handful of dandelion heads into the vat, causing it to flicker in and out of existence the way the time collection jar and the Victorian time machine had.

Myron distracted himself from the evil-smelling steam rising above the vat by reminding himself that one day all this would pay off in the form of a saved comics collection.

H.G. Wells came in and explored, her

head bobbing this way and that while she gently sniffed the air and everything else. The stuff in the vat made her sneeze. She eventually sat down under the chair that held the perpetually hot coffee and went to sleep.

"I think all this stuff about time-warping dandelions is bogus," Princess said as she viciously tore the heads off dandelions and threw them into her saucepan. "We're developing muscles for nothing."

"That's a heck of an attitude for a science-fiction reader," Myron said. "And what about the coffee? And the Eskimo Tacos?"

"I'm not sure that's science," Princess said, "or even science fiction. The concept of dandelions warping time seems like real fantasyland stuff to me. Besides, finding a warp in time and actually stockpiling time are two different things. There are other ways to keep coffee hot and ice cream cold."

Though he'd been thinking the same things himself, Myron was irritated by her comments. "Do you think my uncle Hugo would fake those results?" he asked. "Do you think that Victorian time machine was just a special effect?"

"Look at this logically," Princess said. "You've read *Scientific American*. The best guess of the best minds on the planet say that to warp time you need a spinning black hole or a superstring or something like that. You can't just grow a warp engine like a weed."

"Why not?" Myron asked.

"Because you can't."

"How do you know? How does anybody know?" Tired of stirring the time mush as well as arguing, Myron left the paddle standing straight up in it. "Want an Eskimo Taco?" he asked.

"Sure," said Princess. She held up her hands and wiggled her fingers at him. "Sticky fingers, sticky fingers," she said evilly.

Myron nodded, humoring her. Princess could be a lot of fun to argue with, but sometimes he wished she would grow up.

He took two Eskimo Tacos from the box. They were still frozen solid, though he knew they had been sitting in the warm barn for at least the few hours that he and Princess had been working. The dandelions obviously warped time. Myron couldn't wait to try them out on his collection. "Think fast!" he shouted and threw an Eskimo Taco to Princess. He was disgruntled when she caught it one-handed, something he could not have done in a million years.

He ignored her feat and tore open the silver bag his Eskimo Taco came in. Inside was a trough of chocolate filled with a wedge of vanilla ice cream. It was cold and delicious. He was glad the dandelions hadn't made the ice cream taste like spinach.

Myron went back to the vat and used the paddle to stir the time mush one-handed, which was just barely possible. He was developing muscles, anyway. Maybe he'd look like the Spartan if he stirred long enough. Princess came over to pour her dandelion heads into the hopper above the vat and stood there watching him while she licked her Eskimo Taco.

Uncle Hugo came in and dumped the latest

crop of dandelions out of a sack onto Princess's table. "These suckers really grow fast," he said. After hanging the sack on a peg, he looked at the time mush, sniffed it, and even tasted a little on the tip of his finger.

Because of the heat rising from the vat, Myron's Eskimo Taco was melting fast. A white rivulet trickled down his wrist, and Myron licked it off. As he did, he accidentally knocked the stirring paddle against the hopper release. Myron watched with horror as the hundreds of dandelion heads left in the hopper fell into the vat all at once.

"Look out!"·Uncle Hugo cried and leaped for the release.

While he was still in the air, the time mush exploded.

4 TOMORROW'S GHOSTS TODAY

Uncle Hugo seemed to hang in the air for a long time, pinned there by rainbows. He fell slowly to the floor leaving a trail of rainbows, as if he were doing something funny to the air as he passed. There was no sound except a great rushing, like wind through an ancient forest.

Myron knew why Hugo didn't move very fast. When he tried to raise his own hand, Myron found that the air seemed to have turned to glue. His skin tingled as if he were being shocked lightly with electricity, and he couldn't talk at all.

Uncle Hugo was still falling, and Princess was still looking at him in horror. From under her chair, H.G. Wells watched everything with enormous eyes. They could all see each other, but each of them seemed to be staring out from a small separate universe. How long could this go on?

Then Myron noticed something that astonished him even more than his unpleasant condition. In the middle of the room, coexisting in the same space as a table and the Astronetics electronic scrutinizer that stood on it, ghostly full-size images of Princess and himself waved at him frantically. They were difficult to see, little more than gray outlines—like pictures from a TV station with a weak signal. The figures seemed to be standing in a forest clearing next to a pumpkin the size of a four-story building. Nearby was a statue of a cherub posing on top of a column on one toe; he had only one wing in the middle of his back, which gave him a sharklike appearance. Myron had never seen anything like it. He and Princess had moss in their hair, and their hands appeared to have gotten bloaty and lost definition, as if they were wearing gloves filled with sand.

The ghost Myron did not seem surprised to see him; he awkwardly pulled a dandelion from his pocket and pointed at it again and again while mouthing words Myron could not decipher.

Suddenly, the rainbows and the rushing and the tingle were gone, along with the ghosts. Hugo struck the floor hard, almost crushing H.G. Wells, who bolted from the barn like a streak. Princess shrieked, and Myron fell over, unbalanced as he was because of reaching—too late—for the hopper release.

Myron stayed on the floor collecting his wits. Apparently, the others felt as dazed as he did because they each stayed where they were, gaping and breathing hard.

The vat looked as if it had burst at both ends, even the end that had already been open. The green smell was stronger than ever, but the time mush was gone, which was okay with Myron. He was glad not to be covered with the stuff.

"What happened?" Uncle Hugo asked.

"Myron hit the release with his stir stick," Princess explained.

"Thanks a bunch," Myron said.

"He asked," Princess said.

Uncle Hugo stood and stared at the busted vat. "Not a problem," he said. "The course of true science never did run smooth. Not often, anyway. Let's see if we can learn something here." He circled the vat while humming to himself and smiling.

"See?" Myron said to Princess. "We might learn something."

"You lead a charmed life, Duberville," Princess said.

Myron agreed with her, though he wasn't ready to admit it out loud. He also wasn't ready to mention the ghosts, not wanting to find out that he was the only one who'd seen them.

Hugo snapped his fingers. "A time fluctuation," he cried. He got down onto his knees and casually stroked the small puddle of time mush that remained in the vat. "We were lucky," he said.

"Lucky we weren't killed," Princess muttered.

"There's that, of course," Uncle Hugo said, as if their deaths were of little importance. "But I meant we were lucky in a temporal rather than a physical sense."

Myron and Princess waited for him to say more, but apparently Hugo considered his comment to be self-explanatory because, with a thoughtful expression on his face, he silently began to sweep the bits of the vat out the door.

"What do you mean, 'we were lucky in a temporal sense'?" Myron asked.

Uncle Hugo glanced at him in surprise, but he kept sweeping. "We were heating the time mush over a regular chemical fire," he explained. "If we had put more energy into those dandelions—using an atomic furnace, say—those babies could have sent you into the middle of next week."

"What happened to the dandelions?" Princess asked. "All that's left is some muck in the bottom of the vat."

"Washed down the time stream?" Myron suggested.

"That must be what happened to the dinosaurs," Princess cried.

"What?" Myron and his uncle Hugo asked together.

"Washed down the time stream."

"I don't know about the dinosaurs," Uncle Hugo said, "but I believe that Myron is correct about the time mush. Which is just one more reason we have to get this place cleaned up. We have to start another batch right away. All over the world, food is rotting as we speak."

"Wait a minute, Uncle Hugo. I have to ask you something."

"Spit it out, Myron. We have work to do."

Myron had to know, no matter how silly the question made him sound. "I saw ghosts of Princess and me," he said. "The ghosts were draped in moss, and their hands looked like unbaked cookies."

"I saw the same thing," Princess said quietly.

"Then it wasn't a hallucination!" Uncle Hugo said and snapped his fingers again.

"What was it?" Princess asked.

Myron had a thought that made him feel cold and weak all over. "It was us in the middle of next week," he said.

Princess's eyes widened. "You think?" she asked.

Uncle Hugo nodded. "It's possible we just experienced a time warp, where a few moments of our time touched a few moments farther along the time road."

Suddenly, the whole idea of time-traveling dandelions and temporal insulation seemed a lot more real to Myron. The chances of saving his comics collection from decay seemed to have improved, though his chances of surviving to adulthood seemed to have deteriorated. "How far along the time road?" he asked.

"Impossible to say," Uncle Hugo admitted.

"We looked as if we had some weird disease," Princess said.

Uncle Hugo frowned. "Maybe the picture was distorted."

Myron wasn't convinced, and he didn't believe Uncle Hugo or Princess were convinced either. As far as Myron could see, he was destined to have a terrible future. Looking like a moss-covered unbaked cookie was even worse than having zits.

"The ghost-Myron seemed to be telling us about that dandelion he was holding," Princess said. She looked at Myron as if she expected him to remember something that hadn't happened yet.

Princess's unreasonable assumption irritated Myron. "Don't look at me," he said.

"Let's get this place cleaned up," Uncle Hugo said. "Maybe something will come to us while we're working."

The place was such a shambles that knowing where to start was difficult, but soon they were sweeping out bits and setting furniture back on its feet. H.G. Wells returned and helped them by sitting and washing herself on the table where Princess had been decapitating dandelions.

They barely had time to get the barn back

in order before Princess's father arrived to take her home. She was about to open the front door when Myron came into the foyer with H.G. trotting behind.

"Will I see you tomorrow?" Myron asked.

"Absolutely. I think your uncle Hugo's really on to something here."

Myron chuckled. "I thought that explosion might convince you that we're dealing with real science."

"Amazing, huh? See you tomorrow."

Princess ran down the wide front steps of the mansion to where her father was waiting in the family station wagon.

Uncle Hugo had recently had a bad experience with his butler, so despite his wealth he had no servants. He and Myron had to forage for themselves in the vast freezer he kept in a back room off the kitchen. The selection of frozen dinners, pot pies, egg rolls, and pizzas was enormous—larger than might be found in some supermarkets. To Myron, all the frozen food began to taste the same after a while. He suspected that eating it every night was the thing that had driven Uncle Hugo to think about food preservation. In fact, Hugo seemed to meditate over each forkful as he chewed.

Despite Princess's willingness to return the next day, and his own determination to save his comics, the ghostly vision they'd all had continued to prey on him. Instead of falling asleep he lay in the dark wondering how bloated and stringy he could become and still be himself, and whether he would also smell bad, and whether it would affect his brain. What a fate for a guy who used to wear pelican sport shirts!

The next morning, Myron was still worrying about the terrible things the future might hold. He'd pretty much decided that saving his comics collection was not worth becoming the Elephant Kid.

Myron came into the kitchen intending to bring up the matter right away, but he was distracted when he saw Hugo wearing a business suit.

"Nice outfit," Myron said.

Hugo chuckled as he stood at a counter absentmindedly spreading peanut butter on bread. "I'm going to pitch my food preservation ideas to the fogies at Astronetics, and I thought I'd dress for the occasion. I'll infiltrate them," he said and winked. "They're sending a limo. It ought to be here pretty soon."

Myron mixed some water into his instant oatmeal and nuked it in the microwave. "You know, Uncle Hugo," he began, "maybe we shouldn't be doing this."

"Nonsense, my boy. Breakfast is the most important meal of the day." Hugo sprinkled brown sugar onto his peanut butter sandwich.

"No, I mean draining off time, making dandelion mush, any of that stuff."

Uncle Hugo put down his sugar spoon. "Go on," he said.

"The problem," Myron said, "is those ghosts we saw. I don't want to get that weird disease."

Hugo pondered for a moment. "Actually," he said, "I'm glad you brought that up. I've been worrying about that weird disease, too, and I've come to a conclusion. Generally, avoiding one's destiny is either easy or it's impossible."

"Huh?" The microwave beeped. Myron took out his oatmeal and stirred it.

"It's possible that by doing something to avoid a certain situation, you might actually end up causing the situation. Think about crossing the street to avoid getting hit by a falling safe, and then getting run over by a car as you're crossing."

Myron sighed. "Then, as many aliens say, 'Resistance is useless.' "

Uncle Hugo nodded. "You might as well not worry about what you do because nobody knows where any choice leads. We each have to do what seems logical at the time. My advice to you, Myron, is not to worry any more than you have to." He took more peanut butter on his knife, but instead of spreading it on bread, he scraped it off with one finger and then licked off his finger.

Myron felt despondent. Sure, he thought. Go stand in the corner and don't think a hippopotamus. What a joke!

TIME LEAP II

IT IS DAYTIME, BUT AMONG THE TREES OF THE FOREST THE AIR IS DIM AND COOL. THE FOREST CREATURES GO ABOUT THEIR BUSINESS.

A CALICO CAT GAMBOLS LIGHTLY OVER THE FALL OF PINE NEEDLES, STOPS, LOOKS BACK, AND THEN CONTINUES. CRASHING THROUGH THE FOREST A SHORT DISTANCE BEHIND THE CAT IS A LARGE BLOND MAN IN COVERALLS.

BANDOLEERS CARRYING COLORED BALLS CROSS HIS CHEST. HE CARRIES AN ORANGE BALL IN ONE HAND, READY TO THROW. AS HE PURSUES THE CAT THE BIG MAN SINGS A WEIRD SONG, LIKE SOME JOLLY BLOODTHIRSTY ALIEN MARCHING OFF TO WAR.

THE MAN COMES UPON THE CAT, WHO IS WAITING IN A PATCH OF SUNLIGHT. THE MAN CHUCKLES UNPLEASANTLY AND HURLS THE ORANGE BALL AT HER.

THE CAT LEAPS AWAY, AND
THE BALL EXPLODES AGAINST THE
GROUND WHERE SHE HAS BEEN,
LEAVING BEHIND AN AREA
THE SIZE OF A DINNER PLATE
THAT IS NOW ORANGE
AND STRINGY.

A FRAGRANCE OF
PUMPKIN ARISES FROM THE SPOT.
THE MAN ROARS ANGRILY AND
MARCHES AFTER THE CAT
AGAIN.

THE FOREST IS SILENT
FOR AWHILE BEFORE THE SMALL
ANIMALS ONCE AGAIN GO ABOUT
THEIR BUSINESS.

5 THE SMELL OF FEAR

While Myron and Hugo were eating, a strange noise assaulted them from outside. At first it was no more than the faraway whistling of a teakettle, but it soon became a warbling wail that was so loud, they had to put their hands over their ears or be deafened. H.G. Wells leapt into Myron's lap and crouched there as if expecting someone to strike her. The noise went on for a long time, and then stopped so abruptly the silence felt like another kind of sound.

"What was that?" Myron cried.

Neither of them knew, of course, so they left their breakfasts to take a look around. They found Princess at the bottom of the steps gazing at a cloud of dust that hovered over the forest separating Hugo's mansion from the street.

"Come on, Princess," Hugo cried. "You're just in time." He led them into the forest, but they soon stopped when loud pings and bangs and pops came from up ahead. Cautiously, they approached the racket. They stopped at the edge of a clearing and gaped at what stood in the center of it.

"Wow!" Myron said, astonished. "It's a truck."

"Way cool," Princess said.

Hugo grinned and rubbed his hands together. "Amazing! An ancient International Harvester pickup truck!"

The three of them stepped into the clearing for a closer look, but they couldn't get too close because the truck was so hot. Its salmon-pink paint was faded and scuffed. Its bed was empty, but it showed signs of hard use. The windows were too dusty to allow them a look into the dark cab.

"Where did it come from?" Princess asked.

"The sky, maybe?" Myron suggested. He pointed. "See? No tire tracks."

"I don't think it came through time," Hugo said. "The Victorian time machine wasn't hot when it arrived. None of my time collectors ever get hot."

"Outer space, then," Princess said, almost whispering. "It probably heated up dropping through the atmosphere."

"Do you think it's a coincidence, Uncle Hugo?" Myron asked.

Hugo stared at the truck, arms crossed, shaking his head. "Er, what?" he asked.

"The time machine, the dandelions, the exploding mush, and now this?"

"I have no idea. I'm still stunned. I didn't even know they *drove* pickup trucks out there." He squinted up at the sky.

"I don't believe in coincidences, myself," Princess said.

"Me neither," Myron said.

As the metal cooled, the banging slowed and then stopped altogether. They continued to circle the truck like wary animals until a sudden loud squeak froze them. They gathered at the driver's door, which was now open a crack. Myron held his breath.

Even before the thing inside the truck emerged, Myron could smell it. It smelled like a fish market—or like the beach when the tide was out. Myron knew the smell would soon get on his nerves.

The door squealed loudly when it opened, as if it hadn't been oiled for a long time. A big human guy descended from the truck but came no closer to them, which was all right with Myron because of the smell. He had a square face and short blond hair, and wore gray coveralls. Bandoleers criss-crossed his chest, as if he were a movie Mexican bandit. Instead of holding bullets or hand grenades, the bandoleers held what looked like golf balls in assorted colors.

The guy turned his head slowly with the heavy, frightening inevitability of a tank turret, and when he glared at them he giggled. Maybe the giggle was meant to be friendly, but to Myron it was a mirthless psychotic sound rattling around the bottom of a loony bin.

"Don't be shy," Uncle Hugo said calmly.

"Why should I be?" the man asked as if he'd been insulted. "No, I'm not Shy. I'm A.L." He pointed to the pocket of his gray coveralls as if to prove it. Embroidered there was *A.L.*, just like that, with a period after each letter.

A.L. lifted his hands and waved them slowly through the air as if he were parting a curtain, and then widened his stance. He stopped in that position. "I come in peace," he said. He slowly returned to his original position and ran a hand down one of his bandoleers. All the time he watched Myron. The motions suggested a great deal of power under tight control. Tangling with A.L. would end the same way as arguing with a polar bear.

"Welcome to the Earth," Uncle Hugo said. He held out his hand to be shaken. "I'm Hugo Duberville. This is my nephew Myron and his friend Princess."

A.L. ignored Uncle Hugo's hand. Still fingering the golf-ball things, A.L. turned and stared as if Myron were a bug under a microscope. A.L. unbuttoned one of his breast pockets and from it took a flat black case no larger than Myron's wallet. From the case, he unfolded what looked like a miniature radar dish, an old-fashioned mechanical eggbeater, and three different kinds of knives. He lifted a lid on the top, releasing a crowd of mechanical eyes, each the size of a baseball. The eyes hovered around Myron like a cloud of insects, causing him to retreat. The eyes followed.

"Get those things off me!" Myron demanded.

"They're just looking," A.L. said.

"You're bothering the boy," Uncle Hugo said.

"Am I?" A.L. asked innocently. "Oh.

Sorry." He chuckled again in his insane way, and slowly, as if he were practicing a ballet move, he waved the case through the air. The eyeballs streamed back into it along with the radar dish and the knives.

"Myron and I will be very good friends," A.L. said. "Oh, yes, we will." He grinned in a way Myron found upsetting, perhaps because A.L. continued to stare at him. Myron was accustomed to being ignored by adults when another adult was around.

"You didn't come all this way to see Myron," Uncle Hugo said.

A.L. seemed astonished. "Oh, no?" he said. While he spoke, he glanced at the eggbeater. A red light on top had begun to flash. A.L. roared like an angry lion and set off through the forest, following the eggbeater as if it were some kind of detector.

Uncle Hugo ran after him. Princess glanced at Myron with an unhappy expression on her face. Suspecting that he'd lost his mind entirely, he ran after Uncle Hugo. Princess jogged along beside Myron.

Following A.L. was not difficult because he crashed straight through the forest, detouring only for major trees. He bullied through mere bushes, skittered over boulders like a lizard, and frightened entire flocks of birds that made the sound of applause as they flapped into the air and wheeled over the forest.

A.L. roared again as Myron and Princess came upon him and Uncle Hugo. The eggbeater light was flashing like mad. Standing in the middle of the path, facing them, was H.G. Wells, the cat. She hissed threateningly, and her hackles were up.

A.L. giggled. "So, we meet again," he said. He and H.G. circled each other. Then, with the single whirlwind movement of a major league pitcher, A.L. pulled an orange golf ball from a bandoleer and flung it at H.G.

"No!" Myron, Princess, and Hugo all cried together.

H.G. screamed in a way that sounded frighteningly human and leapt at A.L. As the orange golf ball struck the ground where

H.G. had been, H.G. climbed A.L. as if he were a tree. He tried to grapple with her, but in seconds she was on top of his head, from which she leapt into the forest and disappeared. Where the orange golf ball struck, it left what appeared to be a small puddle of stringy orange stuff.

Uncle Hugo strode to the puddle and peered in the direction H.G. had gone. He turned to A.L. "What was that all about?" he asked angrily.

A.L. just chuckled as he picked up the eggbeater. It was flashing very slowly now. "We have fur balls where I come from, too," he said.

"But they're not—" Princess began.

"A fur ball is a fur ball," A.L. said.

"We kind of got the idea you knew this particular fur ball from someplace," Myron said.

A.L.'s eyes narrowed, and he got cagey. "Fur ball reminded me of somebody I knew," he said.

"This is pumpkin p'yugch," Uncle Hugo

said. He was kneeling next to the orange puddle.

"*P'yugch?*" Myron asked. Pronouncing the word was like clearing your throat.

"The wet stringy stuff that comes inside pumpkins," Hugo said. "You would have done this to our cat?" he asked A.L. "Turned him into p'yugch?"

"Sure. No more fur." A.L. plucked another orange ball from a bandoleer and tossed it casually in one hand while he stared after H.G. The ball gave off sparks as it rose and fell.

"Leave the cat alone," Uncle Hugo ordered.

"Boinks work on humans, too," A.L. said threateningly. He turned to Myron. "This shouldn't take long." He poked Myron with a thick finger. "You stay here till I come back. And don't go near my truck!"

"Whatever you say, sir," Myron said.

"I can't hear you!" A.L. shouted into his face.

"I can sure hear you!" Myron shouted back, surprising himself.

But A.L. only patted him gently on the head. "That's fine," he said and laughed crazily. Then, using his eggbeater as a guide, he marched into the forest after H.G., stiff and powerful as a big robot.

"You kids try to stay out of trouble," Uncle Hugo said as he followed A.L.

When they were out of sight, Myron and Princess ran back to the salmon-pink International Harvester pickup truck. He leapt onto the running board to peer through the windshield under his hand.

"We should have gone with your uncle Hugo instead of coming here," Princess said. "He and H.G. might need help."

"I think we can help them more by finding out all we can about A.L.," Myron said as he tried another window. "Who he is, where he's from, why he's interested in me—that kind of thing. The fact that he ordered us not to go near this truck means that we *must* search it." He hopped down from the running board and studied the object of their interest. Myron decided he would actually rather search A.L.'s truck than run into him alone. Though, in his view, it was a poor choice.

"You're just afraid of A.L.," Princess said.

"It seems like the rational reaction, all things considered."

Princess grinned at him and climbed onto the running board. She made a grab for the handle, but Myron pushed her aside. "This isn't really your problem," Myron said, feeling both noble and stupid.

"Hogging all the glory?" Princess asked.

"Suit yourself." He pushed in the button and found to his dismay that the handle turned easily. It figured—everything else had gone wrong that day. The hinges groaned loudly as he pulled the door open. Without entering, he and Princess peered inside and, to their surprise, saw only the cab of an old International Harvester truck. A.L.'s distinctive smell flooded out at them.

The seat was a single padded couch covered in cracking plastic of some dark color. There were pedals on the floor and a big black steering wheel, and on the dash was a row of silver knobs. A heap of small electronic parts filled the ashtray. The glove box was held closed by a length of wire. A stick shift with rubber bands around it rose from the center of the floor.

Princess slid across to the passenger's side of the seat. With his heart pounding, Myron climbed into the truck and sat behind the wheel. While Princess untwisted the wire holding the glove box closed, Myron slammed the door.

What he saw took his breath away.

6 CLUES

When the door slammed, the cab disappeared and with it the wire Princess had been holding. Myron and Princess were still sitting on the same couch, but now it was at one end of a big room.

Resting delicately on the deck near the center of the room was a big ball of water many feet across; the top was lost in shadows high above the deck, up where onion fans turned. Except where ripples broke the surface, the ball was perfectly round, and so big that it looked like a planet somebody had dragged indoors. Dim lights on the sides of dark swimming shapes cast spidery patterns that constantly changed on the walls, deck, and ceiling, making the room seem mysterious. Dotted across the deck around the water planet were frameworks, machines of some kind. The place smelled as bad as A.L. Not a surprise.

"Wow," Princess commented. "Awesome."

Myron was not yet ready to make a value judgment on the interior of A.L.'s truck. "What does it all mean?" he asked.

"A.L. knows something about gravity that we don't?"

"I was thinking more like we should have brought diving gear."

"Even if we only search the dry parts," Princess said, "I think we'll be here for a while."

Myron could see that Princess was right. Still, they had to begin. A.L. could be back any minute, and he would certainly not be sympathetic to their need for information. Myron forced himself to stand. He and Princess moved quickly across the deck.

"I once read about a place like this in a Spartan adventure," he said. "In the story, outside the building was some weird other-dimensional place."

"Science-fiction novels are full of locations like this, too," Princess agreed. "If this room was in the clearing, we would have seen the outside of it in the clearing."

They stopped near one of the frameworks. It had a seat and six grips at the ends of long poles. To Myron, six seemed at least four too many.

"Exercise machine or instrument of torture?" Princess asked.

"Next, on Roving Eye News."

They both laughed uneasily.

They were moving on to the next machine when a whooshing sound startled them. They looked around frantically and saw a fleet of boinks diving toward them from the shadows near the ceiling. Myron watched, fascinated, until something hit him in the back, shoving him to the deck just as the boinks zoomed over. Princess was on her belly next to him. Myron glanced up and saw the boinks circling for another run.

"Lie still," Myron said.

"I don't get any stiller," Princess assured him.

The boinks zoomed over them three more times and then went away. Myron lay on the cold deck for as long as he could, sweating, knowing that he and Princess were wasting valuable time. He looked around and then got to his feet. Princess stood up next to him.

"Thanks for saving me," Myron said as they began to explore again.

"No biggie," Princess said. "How'd you know the boinks would go away if we didn't move?"

"I didn't. It was more like wishful thinking."

They were attacked by boinks twice more before they reached the far side of the room. Each time, lying still on the deck saved them.

On the far side of the room they found a workbench and a tall metal cabinet. The cabinet had no doors or handles, but the scratching noises and the occasional growl that issued from within made that all right with Myron.

"I hope the doorknob isn't on the *inside*," Princess said.

A rack was attached to the side of the cabinet. It held more boinks, in orange, blue, green and yellow—a whole row of each.

"He looks as if he's ready for anything," Myron said.

The objects on the workbench were laid out with care, like a surgeon's instruments. Small metal insects, obviously electronic components, were lined up in neat rows. Behind them were baskets, each containing a different kind of alien fruit or vegetable. They might have been components, too. The workbench was clean, and the deck around it had been swept recently.

"Parts," Myron said.

"Yeah. Spaceship parts. Time machine parts."

Myron was alarmed when Princess put out

a hand to pick up one of the metal insects. "Don't touch anything," he said. "This guy looks as if he's really compulsive. He'll notice if we don't put something back just right."

Princess wiggled her fingers over the work-bench as if she really wanted to touch something, but she nodded and lowered her hand. "Takes one to know one, huh, Myron?"

"What? Listen: I may be neat, but this guy is a psycho."

"OK. I see the difference. Don't get your pelicans in an uproar. What, exactly, are we looking for?"

"I don't know." He glanced around, hoping he'd recognize a clue when he saw one. They had to hurry. "Something to tell us more about A.L. Something that'll connect him to me. Something like—*that*." He pointed to a poster over the workbench that showed an enlargement of a comic book page; it featured a piglike alien packing a futuristic pistol that hurled concentric rings of light. When the rings hit something, the target glowed brighter and brighter until it exploded into sparks. Apparently, the only thing that could stop the pig's ring finger was a power glove used by the hero, who in this case happened to be the Spartan. On command, the glove cracked great whips of light that scattered the rings. The page rose into the gloom.

"Maybe A.L. is a collector, too," Princess said.

"I guess so. He's collecting *my* comic books."

"So?" she said and shrugged. "Anybody can collect Spartan comics."

"You don't understand. It's not just an enlargement from the same issue—it's from *my copy*."

Princess blinked at him. "That's pretty amazing," she said, "if true."

"Look at this." Myron took a pen from his pocket and pointed to a small stain in one corner of the page. "This has to be an enlargement of a page from one of the books I bought from that guy's mother. I remember thinking that this stain looks kind of like a horse's head."

Princess peered at the stain. "How would A.L. get an enlargement of a page in a comic book that's up in your room?" she asked.

"*How* doesn't bother me as much as *why*."

Princess nodded. "Not to mention the fact that A.L. gives us both the flying zambeenees. I don't know about you, Myron, but I find all this just the teensy-weensiest bit suspicious."

"As far as I'm concerned, he's been acting suspicious since he got here, and it scares me."

"I'm pretty scared myself, even though A.L. doesn't seem to have any interest in *me*."

"He might stir some up if he finds us here."

Without quite knowing how he began, he and Princess were running back to the couch. They were about even with the water planet when they heard the cry of the cab door opening.

They froze. Terrified, Myron wanted to run. But he did not know where to go.

7
A
COMIC
BOOK
LIFE

Princess took Myron's hand, which surprised him almost as much as the sudden noise, and pulled him into the darkness at one side of the room. The rippling edge of the water planet loomed near them.

From their hiding place, Myron saw a door-shaped area open in the air, through which he could see the clearing. He also saw the ghostly outline of the truck's cab. A.L.

climbed into the cab, slammed the door, and leapt to his feet with his fists clenched.

"Where are you?" he shouted. Then he giggled and tiptoed farther into the room. "Come out, come out, wherever you are," he called.

If they needed more evidence that A.L. was a psycho, here it was. What would the Spartan do in a case like this? He glanced at Princess. She seemed to be as wide-eyed with fear as he was. Though the room was not warm, sweat rolled down his sides from under his arms. Myron burned to know if A.L. had done something terrible to H.G. or to Uncle Hugo.

A.L. strode to one of the machines. "I told you to stay put, but you didn't," he said in a wheedling voice. He hit the framework of the machine with his fist, making it resound like a gong. "I know you're in here," he cried. "Resistance is useless!"

He began to search frantically throughout the room, sometimes giggling, sometimes yelling threats. Because he ran from one end of the room to the other, looking here and there seemingly as the spirit moved him, he missed a lot of places—one of them the shadow in which Myron and Princess huddled and sweated. Eventually, in frustration, A.L. lifted one framework over his head and threw it at another. They clanged together and made a tangled wreck.

After throwing the framework he stood before the water planet breathing hard. A moment later, A.L. did something that astonished Myron so much he forgot his fear.

A.L. stood at ease before the water planet. With the air of a man unbuttoning his shirt after a long day, he shrugged off his bandoleers and ran one hand down the front of his coveralls. The coveralls disappeared, along with his human head and his human hands.

He shook loose a few tentacles that were bundled to make a right leg, then shook loose a few more that made his left. More tentacles made his arms. Big round eyes looked out from under a fringe of tiny thin tentacles that wiggled constantly like worms. Beneath the eyes was the inverted V of his mouth. A.L.'s skin was a dark mottled brown; it was slick, like the body of a wet seal. About where his pocket had been, some of the dark spots spelled out *A.L.* He casually braided his arm tentacles and pushed them away from himself, like a man cracking his fingers.

A.L. was not some guy but a slimy terror from beyond space! The revelation seemed so preposterous that for a moment Myron found it difficult to accept. But the evidence continued to writhe before his eyes.

Then, with the grace of an animal at home in the water, A.L. slid up into the water planet. Immediately, the fishy shapes that had been swimming so placidly began to thrash around, splashing water in all directions. The water arced and fell to the deck. The water wasn't chlorinated, as Myron had expected, but smelled like seawater—*alien* seawater.

The smaller shapes scattered as A.L.'s big dark shape glided swiftly through the water. Then he leapt into the air at an impossible angle, water coursing off him and gripping a gray fishy thing that flapped madly in his mouth. He spit the fish onto the deck and fell back into the water, making a bigger splash than before. The fish flopped for a while but soon stopped. A.L. brought fish after fish to the surface and spit it onto the deck.

Myron glanced at Princess. She was staring at the water planet in horror. She glanced at Myron, her eyes still wide, and then back at the water planet.

With one clean motion, A.L. leapt free of whatever field held the water planet in place and, like a gymnast, landed next to it dripping as his tentacles curled gently from side to side. He suddenly roared like a sea lion, shook himself like a wet dog, and grabbed the nearest dead fish. Though the fish was bigger than a loaf of bread, A.L. opened his mouth wide and took it all in at once. He seemed to swallow it without even chewing. He kicked the many other fish aside as he walked to the workbench, dripping a wet trail behind on the deck.

He grabbed a handful of green boinks and,

faster than Myron's eye could follow, threw them at the dead fish, making each one catch fire and fizz like a Fourth-of-July sparkler. When a fish finished sparkling, it was gone.

When the floor was empty again, A.L. slowly turned his head, scrutinizing the room. Myron swore that A.L. looked right at him, but A.L. only turned to the work-bench and barked at the cabinet. It sprang open. From inside he pulled out a flashlight, an object too small for Myron to see, and what he thought was a weapon until A.L. pulled a small movie screen from the side of its barrel and stood it on a tripod.

"Ardath Ludusko calling Marsy Batter," A.L. said as he stood stiffly before the blank screen; just the tips of his tentacles curled and uncurled. "Ardath Ludusko calling Marsy Batter."

"Ardath Ludusko must be what *A.L.* stands for," Myron said, pleased by his own cleverness.

"All right, smart guy, who's Marsy Batter?" Princess whispered.

"Who wants to know?" Myron asked,

wishing he had the answer to Princess's question.

For a moment, the screen showed nothing but electronic snow and jagged bands of color, but soon a lightning bolt formed diagonally on the screen. The bolt slid apart to show a grandmotherly woman with a grim, immobile face. She had gray hair combed straight back and gathered into a neat bun. Her eyes held a cold intelligence. She hadn't yet said or done anything, but Myron was immediately even more afraid of her than he was of A.L.

"Marsy Batter here," the woman said in a quiet, firm voice that was supremely confident. "Report."

"I found The Myron," A.L. said.

Myron gulped and squeezed Princess's hand.

"Very good," Marsy Batter said. "Care must be taken to extract him from the time stream in a way causing the least possible turbulence. There must be no witnesses."

"He has friends," A.L. said uneasily.

Myron was sure he didn't want to meet the person who could make A.L. uneasy.

"Deal with them."

"One of them is a fur ball."

Marsy Batter blinked at A.L., but her expression didn't change. "That is unfortunate. Use the orange boink."

"Right. Right."

Myron noticed that A.L. didn't tell her he'd already tried an orange boink on H.G., and missed.

"Because of the presence of the fur ball we must advance our timetable," Marsy Batter said. "You will plant the pumpkin now."

"I haven't finished my reconnaissance."

"You will plant the pumpkin now," she said again without raising her voice. "Take steps to see that The Myron does not escape. Marsy Batter, out."

The sides of the lightning bolt came together like a shutter, and the interference returned to the screen.

A.L. chuckled as he let the screen down into the barrel like a window shade and put it back into the cabinet. He sighed as he climbed back into his human disguise, grabbed the flashlight and the thing that was too small to see, and marched across the deck to the beat of a rhythmic series of guttural noises that might have been singing. The music was medieval and spooky, the kind of song Myron had heard in nightmares. It echoed in the big room. A.L. stopped suddenly in the middle of the floor and peered around again.

Myron held his breath.

A.L. returned to the couch, sat down, opened the truck's door, and went out. The door slammed behind him.

Myron let out his breath.

"What was that all about?" Princess cried.

"Me," Myron said forlornly. "Somebody named Marsy Batter sent A.L. to do something horrible to me with a pumpkin."

"I don't know, Myron, being threatened with a pumpkin doesn't sound very serious."

"A thing doesn't need rivets and an atomic

generator to be dangerous, Princess. Look at what those boinks can do."

Princess sighed. "You're right. I was trying to lighten up a little, but A.L. and Marsy Batter *do* look as if they're playing for keeps. What I don't understand is, why you?"

"You know as much as I do." Myron was doomed. How could Princess, or even Princess and Uncle Hugo together, help him against a slimy terror from beyond space—whether it was using a pumpkin or not?

"We have to follow him," Princess said.

"Why? Maybe I should just wait here to be pumpkined and save everybody a lot of trouble."

"Not pumpkined, Myron. *Squashed.*"

"Go ahead. Make jokes."

"Somebody has to make jokes. Your argument is bogus, and you know it. What would the Spartan say about giving up?"

Myron considered. He and Princess seemed to be in over their heads this time. But they'd been in over their heads before and had come out all right. Besides, if he was going to be captured anyway, he had nothing to lose by attempting to remain free. Besides again, he didn't want to look like a coward in front of a girl.

He took a deep breath. "All right," he said. "Let's boogie."

They walked to the couch, giving the water planet a wide berth. Myron sat down on the driver's side and felt around for the door handle.

Princess sat down beside him. "Wait," she whispered. Myron waited. The door would make an incredible noise when it moved, and if A.L. was anywhere near he would hear it. Yet, if he got too far ahead of them, they'd never be able to follow. It was a touchy situation, no question.

Myron waited as long as he could, then he gently pushed down on the door handle. When he felt the door give, he pushed it open as slowly as he could, causing it to creak a little. He stopped.

"Go ahead," Princess whispered.

"He'll hear us."

"We'll lose him."

Myron pushed the door open a little farther, and through part of the motion it made no noise at all. At the point where it stuck, he stopped again and slid backward out the door through the narrow opening. He stepped onto the running board and then to the ground, grateful that he had escaped. A.L. was nowhere to be seen.

The sun was high in the sky, and shadows huddled under the things that made them. He and Princess would have to be careful if they wanted to stay out of A.L.'s sight.

Princess stood behind Myron on the running board. While he knelt to see if he could find footprints, she carefully closed the truck's door. The air was hot and dry and smelled of dust.

"Find anything?" she asked.

He pointed at large corrugated prints that led into the forest.

"That's him, all right," she said. "Let's blow this Popsicle stand."

She strode off, but Myron didn't move.

"What now?" she asked.

"Maybe we should talk to Uncle Hugo first. He may have an idea what to do about A.L."

"Myron, I like your uncle Hugo a lot, but I don't think he's any more equipped to handle A.L. than we are."

"That's encouraging."

"What I mean is, he's not here and we are. We *can* handle A.L. as well as he can."

Uncle Hugo himself stopped the discussion by emerging from the forest. He was smiling and carrying H.G. Wells like a baby. White cat hairs now lightly dusted the front of his dark suit. Myron and Princess ran to them, pleased that they were all right.

"What happened to you guys?" Myron asked as he took H.G. and scratched her behind the ears.

"Yeah," Princess said, "we were worried that A.L. got you."

Uncle Hugo shook his head. "A.L. wasn't interested in me, and he never did find H.G. Truth is, I had trouble finding her myself. What are you kids up to? With A.L. lurking around, you're safer back at the house. He seems to have an unhealthy interest in Myron."

"Uncle Hugo," Myron said, "you don't know the half of it about A.L. We went into his truck—"

Down by the street a car honked shave-and-a-haircut.

"That must be the limo," Uncle Hugo said. "I asked them to honk. Listen, you kids promise that you'll go back to the house and stay there. We'll figure out this A.L. stuff when I get home."

"But A.L.—" Myron began again.

"Later," Hugo called to them as he ran toward the street. "Go back to the house!" He disappeared among the trees.

"I guess Hugo's an adult after all," Princess said.

"Yeah. A kid's business is never as important as their own. Well, let's go."

"Right," Princess said as they set off.

They hadn't gone far when they lost A.L.'s

trail. The ground was littered with many years' fall of pine needles, and they didn't take a footprint very well.

"What now?" Princess asked.

H.G. struggled out of Myron's arms and leapt lightly to the ground. She padded a few feet away and sat down to face them.

Myron thought about A.L.'s reaction to her and what Marsy Batter had said—that her presence was "unfortunate." That was good enough for Myron. "She wants us to follow her," he said. "I think we should."

"I don't have a better idea," Princess said.

"All right, H.G. Go."

Tail high, H.G. marched off with Myron and Princess right behind her. She seemed to know where she was going, because she walked through the forest without hesitation. How she knew, Myron could not guess. She never even stopped to sniff.

After walking a long distance across Hugo's huge estate, they came to another clearing. Myron, Princess, and H.G. watched from behind a tree as A.L. stood in the center of it looking around. Myron expected A.L.

to just sparkle and disappear, but instead he twisted the head of the flashlight, aimed it at the ground, and switched it on. It started to buzz, and the purple light that hit the ground kicked up dirt.

While A.L. dug a hole with the beam from his flashlight, Myron noticed a statue at one side of the clearing. It astonished him.

He pointed. "Look," he whispered to Princess. "It's that shark cherub." He derived no comfort from finding the place where their diseased ghosts had stood. Or *would* stand. Time travel really messed up your tenses.

Princess's eyes widened. "Could there be another one of those statues?" she whispered.

"I suppose," he admitted. "But I've never seen one. Look."

A.L. turned off his flashlight, then threw something—a seed, maybe—into the shallow hole he'd dug. Before covering the seed with loose dirt, he flung a handful of something into the hole after it. The stuff sparkled like fairy dust. A.L. got down on his knees and filled in the rest of the hole with dirt.

To Myron's horror, H.G. Wells stepped

delicately into the clearing. He tried to grab her, but she was too quick for him. Myron gripped Princess's arm. "What'll we do?" he whispered.

Before Princess had a chance to answer, A.L. quickly rose to his feet and flung an orange boink at H.G. The cat easily scampered out of the way.

A.L. growled and dived into the forest after H.G.

"Come on," Myron said, and ran into the clearing. "H.G. is giving us our chance." For a moment he stared at the dirt, wondering if it would give him the dread disease. He knew it would soil his hands. But when Princess got down on her knees and began to dig, he joined her on the ground. They didn't have much time. A.L. would certainly be back soon.

The dirt had been warmed by the sun and was actually pleasant to play around with, which came as something of a shock to Myron. He never thought he'd see the day when he didn't mind getting dirty. At the bottom of the hole, they found an old dry seed.

"My botany's a little weak," Myron said, "but I've carved enough jack-o'-lanterns to know a pumpkin seed when I see one."

Princess agreed. "Do you think this is the seed Marsy Batter told A.L. to plant?"

"It's a pumpkin seed, and A.L. planted it," Myron said reasonably. He closed it in his fist while he considered taking it with him and incinerating it in the mansion's fireplace.

"We have to let it grow," Princess said. "That's probably the only way we'll find out what it really is."

"I'm not sure I *want* to know what it really is," Myron said. But he let her drop the seed back into the hole and cover it up.

They had just stood up when H.G. raced through the clearing. A.L. ran after her in hot pursuit, but when he saw Princess and Myron he stopped, glanced after H.G., and then chuckled at them in his unpleasant way. "Fancy seeing you kids way out here," he said. He took a black boink from a bandoleer and tossed it in one hand. Myron did not enjoy watching the boink, but he couldn't help himself.

"You kids are pretty smart. Yes, you are."

"We do OK in school," Myron said cautiously. First he had been afraid that A.L. would kill him, but now he was afraid that A.L. wouldn't. There were worse things than a quick clean death, and one of them obviously had to do with pumpkins.

"School," A.L. said, and laughed. "How long have you kids and that fur ball been following me?"

"We weren't following you," Princess said. "We were just out for a walk."

"I think we'll go with Plan B," A.L. said as he backed away from them.

Myron had wanted A.L. to leave, but his backing away had an ominous look.

"Plan B," A.L. said. "Yes, indeed. Plan B."

He made a mysterious pass through the air with his free hand—the hand not tossing the black boink. *Run*, Myron told himself. *Get away!* But he stood there gripping Princess's arm.

With a grunt, A.L. pulled a stem from the black boink using his teeth, releasing a small spout of sparks. Smiling crazily around the stem, he lobbed the boink in their direction, making the sparks fan out behind. Myron wondered what A.L.'s real mouth was doing under the disguise.

The boink landed a few feet away, and as Myron shook off his trance and turned to run, it exploded, blowing him into darkness.

TIME LEAP III

THE SINISTER OLD WOMAN GROWS IN HER PUMPKIN P'YUGCH POD. OUTWARDLY SHE SEEMS TO BE SLEEPING, BUT HER MIND IS BUSY.

ON THE INSIDE OF HER EYELIDS PLAYS A SCENE RELAYED TO HER FROM THE MONOTONOUS COUNTRY OUTSIDE HER PUMPKIN.

GAMELY WALKING ACROSS THE GRAY WASTES ARE TWO CHILDREN IN THEIR EARLY TEENS, A BOY AND A GIRL.

IF WE COULD READ THEIR MINDS, WE WOULD FIND THAT THEY ARE TIRED, HUNGRY, AND AFRAID.

THE TWO TEENAGERS BRIEFLY
STOP TO DISCUSS A SMALL PLOT OF
DANDELIONS HALF-HIDDEN BY A CLOUD OF
LOW-LYING FOG, AND THEN WALK ON. SOON
THEY TOP A RISE AND SEE A PUMPKIN.
THEY CAN'T TELL HOW BIG IT IS,
BUT THEY DON'T HESITATE
APPROACHING IT.

THEIR APPROACH MAKES
THE MOUTH OF THE SINISTER
OLD WOMAN TWITCH.

SHE HAS EVERY REASON
TO SMILE. ONE WAY OR ANOTHER,
THE BOY WILL SOON BE WORKING
FOR HER.

8 ESCAPE VELOCITY

The darkness swirled away, seeming to dissolve in the air, to reveal a rolling gray plain whose monotony was broken only by occasional low-lying patches of luminous yellow fog. The sky was as gray as the rolling plain, but lines of color bloomed and faded across it like fireworks, in ever-changing patterns.

Myron was stunned for a moment.

"Are you OK?" Princess asked. She was

standing a few feet away from him, just as she had been before A.L. threw the boink.

"If you call being here OK," Myron said. "Where are we?" He kicked at the thin layer of gray grit that covered some hard material.

"Wherever a black boink sends you when it does its thing."

Myron nodded. Princess's answer was as good as any he had. "I don't think much of Plan B," he said.

"From what I knew about Plan A, it wasn't so great either."

"Hello!" Myron cried, hoping to attract someone's attention, though he and Princess seemed to be very much alone. His cry fell dead against his ears as if he were in a sound-proof room. He turned slowly to see if any part of the horizon was different from the rest.

"What's that?" he asked as he pointed to a glow that seemed to be coming from one place just over the horizon.

"All-night diner?" Princess suggested. "Radioactive lake? Airport? Fairies?"

"Grand opening?" Myron added.

They marched off toward the light.

The air did its job, but grudgingly. Aside from the fact that it smelled like a closet that had been closed for years, it had no character; it was as monotonous and tasteless as the landscape.

They discovered that every patch of ground fog they saw was gently illuminated by the heads of dandelions growing in the thin soil. Whether the flowers made the fog or the fog caused the dandelions, they did not know.

Princess picked a few and studied them carefully. She handed them to Myron.

"They're all the same," he said. So, they were time dandelions after all. "I would have guessed we were on another planet, but with those dandelions and only those dandelions here, the chances are better that we are screwed up somehow in time."

"Outside time, I think."

"Outside? Sure. Could be. I saw a story once about a guy who stole a time machine and ended up in this place with all these slimy half-melted monsters. The big question is: how do we get back inside? The story in the comic book just ended with the guy stuck there."

"My science-fiction novels have an answer," Princess said. "If you want to hear it."

"Fascinate me," Myron said.

"Think of it this way," she suggested. "Usually, we all travel at one second per second along the road of time in our little car we call the universe. In front of us is all the time we haven't used yet. Behind us is time we *have* used—or as they say in the used car business, the time is pre-owned. Now we're somewhere on that road, but we're not in our car anymore. Or maybe we're not even on the road at all anymore but off to one side."

"That's it? That's the big answer?"

"Give me a break, Myron. We just got here."

Myron laughed suddenly. "That black boink of A.L.'s?" he said. "It was a time bomb."

"Good one, Myron. Very useful."

Myron had no retort. But while they stared at the dandelions, he had an encouraging thought. "If we're in the future," he said, "all we have to do is wait for our little universal car to catch up."

"Not necessarily. My guess is, now that we're here, we're also moving at one second per second."

"You mean the universal car will always be the same distance—er, time, behind us?"

Princess nodded. "Or in front of us," she said. "We'll need some sort of time machine to get home."

They continued to discuss the possibilities, more to hear the sounds of their own voices than to settle a point. Morosely, Myron wondered which way was the future. How did one point to the past? If the road of time was to one side or the other, where was it? As hopelessness overwhelmed him, his anger at A.L. grew. The guy might as well have shot each of them through the head.

Suddenly Myron became excited thinking

about a theory he'd concocted. "Wait a minute, Princess. Remember when the vat of time mush exploded? Uncle Hugo said that if more energy had been available, some terrible time accident would have happened."

"That didn't come out of any comic book," Princess said.

"The point is this," Myron said. "After a few minutes, we dropped back into that universal car of yours because the explosion didn't kick us hard enough; we didn't reach escape velocity."

Princess smiled. "You mean like a rocket ship," she said. "It has to be going fast enough to overcome the Earth's gravitational field or it will fall back. The vat explosion didn't kick us hard enough to entirely escape our own time, so we fell back."

"But when that black boink of A.L.'s exploded, we *didn't* fall back." The challenge of getting his mind around their problem distracted him from his despair. He still didn't see a solution, but if he and Princess could understand the problem, maybe they could find one.

"If you're right, maybe we don't need a time machine to get home," Princess suggested. "A.L. threw us farther than the vat explosion did, but we might fall back into our own universe yet."

"Maybe," Myron said, though he was not optimistic. He didn't think it was wise to count on A.L.'s incompetence to guarantee their escape. On the other hand, A.L.'s self-interest might save them. "I have a feeling that A.L. will come after us before long."

"After *you*, you mean. Don't forget you're The Myron."

"Whatever. If he takes me away from this place, he'll have to take you. I'll make him."

"Bold talk," Princess said. "Besides, even if he does take me, too, all that means is that we'll both be in Marsy Batter's clutches— whoever she is."

Myron began to walk again. They needed a project, any project, he realized—something to keep them busy while they considered their alternatives. "Breakfast happened a long time ago," he said.

"I'm hungry, too."

"That glow is still there. Maybe it *is* an all-night diner."

"We'll have burgers and onion rings and mocha shakes. Calories be damned!" she cried. She looked away, a little embarrassed.

They both knew the chances of finding food here were slim. Eventually they'd probably try eating dandelions, which would certainly be a big mistake. The dandelion mush would stop time in their stomachs, either killing them immediately or turning them into statues. Their guts would be preserved forever while they died of starvation. Horrible. Better or worse than being pumpkined? Myron's mind boggled at the nasty possibilities.

The horizon played tricks on them. Sometimes it seemed so close it was almost under their feet, and sometimes it seemed impossibly far away. The glow was always just beyond.

Their walking became mechanical. Except for slight differences in elevation and the glow over the horizon, everything remained the same. They climbed to the top of a hill, really no more than a gentle rise, and looked down into a shallow valley. They'd grown so used to the fact that the glow was beyond their reach that when they saw its source, they did not notice for a moment. After they noticed, they could barely believe their eyes.

9
THE PUMPKIN ON THE EDGE OF FOREVER

It was a pumpkin. It looked as if it had rolled into the valley like a big marble that had found the lowest place on a warped floor. But it was definitely the source of the glow, and a cloud enveloped it just as the ground fog blanketed the dandelions. The horizon was now as dead as the rest of the landscape.

With nothing to compare it to, and not knowing for certain the distance to the horizon, they could not guess how big the pumpkin was. As they approached, they needed to constantly increase their estimates.

"Marsy Batter ordered A.L. to plant a pumpkin," Myron said.

"I thought that's what he planted in the clearing."

"I thought so, too. Still, this seems awfully coincidental, doesn't it?"

"It does. If that's the pumpkin A.L. planted, what's it for? And how did it get here? And where's here, anyway?"

"You ask many questions," Myron commented.

"Yeah," Princess said, "and not an answer between us."

The pumpkin was pulsing slowly as if it were breathing, or as if it were a big heart. The movement worried Myron. A big prehistoric squash was one thing, but an animal that size was something else altogether.

However, the pumpkin made no threatening moves as Myron and Princess crossed the valley. After a long time, they were close enough to see that the pumpkin was the size of a small house—the outside was, anyway. Because of their experience with A.L.'s truck, Myron knew that insides and outsides did not necessarily match. They walked all the way around the pumpkin and found a doorway with orange stuff hanging over it like a curtain.

"P'yugch," Myron said.

"Makes sense," Princess agreed.

They studied the doorway. They could not see inside, though artificial-looking light shone through the p'yugch and cast a bright rectangle on the gray earth. Small poppings and squealings came through the opening, as if a heap of rubber things were crawling over each other. The p'yugch swayed a little as the pumpkin throbbed, and with every beat the doorway exhaled a strong smell of pumpkin.

"After you, my dear Alphonse," Princess said.

"After you, my dear Gaston," Myron said.

"We sound like a couple of cartoon mice,"

Princess said, but she did not step toward the door.

"This pumpkin is either our big chance to get some answers," Myron said, "or a not very subtle trap. A.L. and Marsy Batter want to do something to me with a pumpkin. A.L. sends us to this place, and we coincidentally run into a pumpkin big enough to hold a dance in. What's your guess?"

"I vote it's a trap."

"That's my vote, too. But we have to take the bait or walk around out here some more, and I've had enough of that." Myron lifted the p'yugch curtain. He expected alarms to go off, but the pumpkin remained quiet except for the pops and squeals.

"They probably expect us to do exactly what you're doing," Princess said.

"Yeah. I hope we can surprise them later."

Myron stepped inside, and the pops and squeals immediately became louder. He stood at the entrance to a huge orange cavern carved entirely from the meat of the pumpkin. P'yugch hung from the walls and ceiling like huge spiderwebs. Each bump and spike that hung from the ceiling gave off light. The inside of the place was in fact much larger than the outside.

Myron had seen photographs of Carlsbad Caverns, with its great rooms—called galleries—with spires rising from the floor and hanging from the ceiling, banks of organ pipes, odd flowers, cities of crystal, rivers, even human faces, all made from stone, all as silent now as they had been for a million years. The main cavern of the pumpkin had some of the same features, and it was impressive. Yet, because of gargoyle shapes crouching all around, and the webs of p'yugch, the main cavern seemed less like a natural wonder than like the main hall of an ancient and long unused castle—an orange castle carved entirely out of pumpkin.

"If anybody's home," Princess said, "his name is Dracula." She was staring in over his shoulder, almost resting her chin on it.

"I'd almost prefer Dracula to A.L. or Marsy Batter," Myron said. "At least we'd know what we were dealing with." The floor was dry. Someone had made paths by scraping off the top layer of p'yugch slime.

"Chemical light," Princess said.

"Yep," Myron agreed. "Like lightning bugs, I guess."

As they walked along a rising path, Myron noticed that the gargoyles tracked them like security cameras in a bank. It felt creepy.

Princess had noticed the gargoyles, too. "Do you think somebody is really watching?" she asked.

"I think it's safer to assume they are. A.L. maybe."

Princess stuck out her tongue at the nearest gargoyle.

"I suppose you think you're being cute," Myron said.

"I suppose I'm pretty scared and humor helps me cope."

Myron nodded sympathetically and stuck out his tongue, too. He felt a little better but not much.

They turned a corner into a long tunnel.

It seemed to Myron that when he came around the corner the walls had been flowing as if alive, but now that he looked at them directly they were stony and unmoving.

"Did you see anything moving along here as we came around the corner?" Princess asked.

"That's a relief," Myron said. "I thought I was going crazy."

"If you are, then so am I." She poked the wall, to no effect. "Optical illusion," she said.

"Sure," Myron said, knowing that neither of them believed it.

At the end of the tunnel they saw something that made them stop and stare in astonishment. It was an enormous pod that hung from a stem the thickness of Myron's arm. Through a layer of p'yugch, Myron saw what looked like a stout old woman wearing a long dress with a patchwork apron over it. She was barefoot and had no hair. Yet she seemed disturbingly familiar.

"I don't like this," Princess said.

Myron was about to agree with her when

each of the woman's feet popped the way white popcorn flowers explode from small yellow kernels, causing a shoe to bloom. She sprouted gray hair that grew back along her head till it was gathered just above the stem into a bun the size of a fist.

The hair on her head made it clear to Myron who the woman was, and knowing filled him with dread. He backed away from the pod. "It's Marsy Batter," he said.

"It looks like her, but when we saw her on A.L.'s screen, she was already complete. This one is still growing. The whole pumpkin is still growing," Princess said as she glanced around. "That must be the squealing: growing parts squeezing past the parts that are standing still."

"All right," said Myron, "I'm impressed. But I don't need another mystery right now. I need some answers."

"And a pizza," Princess added.

"Right. With double cheese and pepperoni. Anything you want. Meanwhile, what do we do with *her*?"

The pod continued to grow and change as Myron and Princess watched. It throbbed in time with the rest of the pumpkin, making the even, steady rising and falling of a sleeping man's chest.

"We could pick her," Princess said, "or drive a stake through her heart." She grimaced with disgust. "Of course, there's a big difference between seeing Dr. Van Helsing puncture Dracula in a movie and doing it myself. I'm not sure I could."

"Yeah. Our choices seem pretty ghastly. And neither one of them seems very sporting."

"You worry about the dumbest things, Myron. These people want to pumpkinize you!"

"We're supposed to be the *good* guys, remember? If we don't worry about 'sporting,' who will?"

"So, what do we do? I didn't bring any handcuffs."

Princess had a point. Desperate situations called for desperate measures. More than once, the Spartan had fooled the bad guy into capturing himself. Still, waiting for Marsy Batter to ripen so they could fool her seemed stupid in the extreme when they had her at their mercy right now.

"All right," Myron said as he grabbed the base of the Marsy Batter pod with both hands. He shuddered, not only because it was slimy and cold, but because what he was doing seemed nasty, unnatural, and even criminal. Knowing that his actions were justified didn't change any of that. "Give me a hand here."

Myron and Princess began to worry the heavy pod up and back, but stopped when they became aware of movement all around them. They stared in horrified fascination as people, seemingly made from pumpkin meat, separated themselves from the walls. They were not finished creations, and each had only the vague outlines of a person. They might have been roughly carved by a three-year-old. Singly and in bunches, they each took a step away from their hiding place against the walls, and turned to face Myron and Princess.

"P'yugch People," Myron said.

"Yeah," Princess said. "That's what we saw flashing."

The army of P'yugch People tottered toward them on stiff legs, holding their arms straight out like movie zombies, their fingers grasping the air.

So the pumpkin was a trap after all. Myron and Princess's confidence in being able to escape seemed foolish now. They dropped the pod and backed a few feet along the tunnel before they turned and ran.

Myron had never found zombies in the movies very convincing—just a cheap way to do horror, he'd thought. But these P'yugch People were really scary. They looked no more intelligent than their movie counterparts, but their large numbers and their mindless approach made Myron feel as if he were under attack by a natural force—by army ants or maybe locusts. Still, the P'yugch People didn't move very fast. Outrunning them should be easy.

"*The Myron*," the P'yugch People moaned. "*The Myron*."

"They seem to know you," Princess said, as she ran beside him.

"Yeah. 'The Myron' is what Marsy Batter called me."

They ran into another gallery, and for a moment Myron thought they were safe. But more P'yugch People were already entering through a tunnel at the far end.

"*The Myron. The Myron*," the P'yugch People moaned as they stumbled forward, their hands grasping the air.

"They're everywhere," Myron cried. "Like cockroaches."

They ran down another tunnel, one that appeared to be empty so far, but Myron doubted they would get away. Whenever a tunnel branched, they chose a route that was not yet overrun by P'yugch People, and hurried deeper and deeper into the pumpkin. Escape became more unlikely all the time, Myron thought desperately. He had no idea where they were, and the number of P'yugch People pursuing them kept growing.

They eventually entered a corkscrew tunnel that curved downward and opened into a wide staircase. At the bottom they found a gallery whose walls flashed with lightning along the strands of p'yugch.

"It's like being inside a brain," Princess said.

There seemed to be no way out except up the staircase they'd come down or through an arch big enough to admit a semitrailer truck; it was closed off by a barrier that seemed to be made of fitted plates of pumpkin shell all radiating from a central point. The plates were pale purple—which was nice, considering all the yellow—and rang like steel when Myron rapped on them with his knuckles.

P'yugch People streamed in from the staircase, closing in for the kill—or at least for the capture. "Don't back into a wall," Myron cautioned. "It might contain more P'yugch People."

Princess nodded. The two allowed themselves to be herded into the middle of the chamber and waited to meet their doom. Thousands of P'yugch People continued to shamble forward, clutching at the air.

"The Myron. The Myron."

10
A CLEAN WELL-LIGHTED PUMPKIN

And then Myron and Princess heard a grating noise coming from the barrier. Myron knew it was too late to do anything, and his heart sank. It had been too late for a long time.

The pumpkin-plates swung into the surrounding wall, and a circular opening grew until it was as large as the arch, allowing Marsy Batter—now out of her pod, or from a different one?—to step into the control chamber. She was smiling in a way that reminded Myron of A.L.

But the smile was the only similarity between them. Where A.L. seemed to have a nervous tic for every occasion, Marsy Batter had a cold calm about her. She moved only when absolutely necessary, and when A.L. might have chuckled psychotically, Marsy Batter's mouth only twitched. If anything, Marsy Batter was even more frightening in her cold than A.L. was in his heat.

"I am pleased to see you," she said levelly.

Myron was to discover that she said everything levelly. He took Princess's hand in his own, and she gripped it hard. *Give only name, rank, and serial number*, Myron thought.

"I am Marsy Batter," the woman said, and bowed so slightly that Myron thought he might have imagined it. "I have a small task I wish you to perform, O Myron. Please come in."

The crowd of P'yugch People parted, making a path to the doorway where Marsy Batter waited. Feeling despair and anxiety so deeply he could barely move, Myron walked across the gallery with Princess at his side.

As they walked, the woman turned and went smoothly into the room beyond. The bare spot beneath her bun showed where she'd snapped off the stem. Her dress was so long he could not see her feet move. She seemed to glide along on ball bearings.

As Myron and Princess walked into the room, the pumpkin-plate barrier irised shut silently behind them.

They were in an old-fashioned living room. Big overstuffed chairs with clawed feet held down the corners of an intricately decorated carpet. Not everything in the room was pumpkin-yellow, but it was all yellowish: butterscotch, sand, yellow-orange—everything from light brown to a bright raincoat color. The many small tables and the mantelpiece were covered with knickknacks and family portraits, photographs of people with crooked-tombstone teeth, eyes that seemed to wander in two directions at once, and heads that were much too small for their bodies. Some of the framed photos showed only body parts, many of which were covered with hair.

"Evidently she's related to the Addams family," Princess whispered.

Marsy Batter turned and studied Myron for a moment, making him squirm. "Please sit down," she said.

Marsy Batter held all the cards. Myron saw no reason to remain standing. He and Princess each took a wingback chair, and in seconds the chairs had spun them into cocoons of p'yugch. Myron struggled and he heard Princess yell, but nothing worked—they were caught, but good. Marsy Batter watched without changing expression.

"By coming here without a guide," she said, "you have shown yourselves to be resourceful, and therefore dangerous. I am taking no chances."

"You're afraid of us," Princess accused.

"You may believe what you wish." Marsy Batter's smile twitched on and off. "I am from

your future," she said, speaking only to Myron. "The far future."

"You travel by pumpkin?" Princess asked
skeptically.

Marsy Batter continued to stare at Myron.
"We have found it to be the most effective
way," she said.

"Fantasyland stuff," Princess muttered
with contempt.

Myron moved a little in his cocoon. The
p'yugch was cold and very strong. To him,
this did not seem like the time to fling insults.
However, Princess's comment seemed to
have no effect on Marsy Batter.

"I understand that you observed A.L.
planting a pumpkin seed," she continued.
"That seed has grown into the pumpkin you
are now aboard."

"But he only planted it a few hours ago,"
Myron said, "and somewhere entirely else."

"We have ways to make a pumpkin grow,"
Marsy Batter explained. "The one seemingly
growing where A.L. planted it is merely
a projection of this one—a sort of three-

dimensional shadow projected into your present. As this pumpkin travels across the graylands, approaching your time from the future, A.L.'s pumpkin will appear to grow larger and more mature."

Myron didn't have to be told what the "graylands" were. It was a perfect name for the desolation he and Princess had crossed getting into this mess.

"We will ride this pumpkin to your present. It will arrive in your time and become ripe in your space simultaneously. I will then readjust the dandelions, and take The Myron to my time."

"What about me?" Princess asked.

"You are of no consequence," Marsy Batter said.

Princess jerked as if she'd been slapped. She looked both relieved and crushed. Myron could understand her mixed feelings. He didn't know which was worse, to be wanted or *not* wanted by Marsy Batter.

"In my time," Marsy Batter said, "I found your box of comic books. Among them is a catalog with the name Myron Duberville on it."

Suddenly Myron saw what had happened. Uncle Hugo's theories about the dandelion mush must have been correct, and he would make (had made?) cardboard out of it. Myron must have stored (would store?) his comics in a dandelionboard box, along with one of the catalogs he was always (would always have been) receiving. (Sheesh, these tenses!) "I still don't know what you want from me," he said.

"Indeed," Marsy Batter said. She crossed her hands over her belly. For the first time Myron saw a ring on her right hand. It looked like a large hunk of crystal cut into the shape of a many-faceted pumpkin. It flashed at him on the rare occasions Marsy Batter moved her hands.

"Those books contain superscience and weapons more advanced than anything I know about. You will build those weapons for me." Marsy Batter spoke as if she'd hired Myron to do a job.

Myron was stupefied. Everything was clear now: A.L.'s interest in him, the enlarged comic book page inside A.L.'s truck, everything. They were being put through this ordeal because Marsy Batter—some vegetable cuckoo from the future—thought comic books were real! It was amazing! It was remarkable! All Myron had to do was explain and everybody could go home.

"No, no, no!" Myron said. "You have it all wrong. Those are *comic* books. Everything in them is made up. None of it is real."

Marsy Batter's smile was supremely and smugly superior. "I expected you to claim something like that, O Myron. Lies will not avail you. You will give me facts and formulas. You will build me weapons. Or you will become my slave forever."

"Wait a minute," Princess said. "Just back up a minute. You have these pumpkins, and P'yugch People, and an arsenal of boinks, and trucks that fly like starships, and stuff we probably haven't seen yet. Even if Myron—*The Myron*—could do what you think, so what? What do you need comic book weapons for?"

"You underestimate The Myron, my dear," Marsy Batter said. "Conquering the universe is not easy. In the future I have many enemies: Lupoff the Magnificent, Ol' Doc Trayne, and the Ineffable Ted! They also have the weapons and other equipment you mention. We are in constant competition for improved military technology. The Myron is my edge."

"But it's *not real*," Myron cried.

Marsy Batter smiled. "I am the judge of what is real and what is not," she said. "Look at your hair. Look at your fingernails." She lifted a finger, and the p'yugch cocoons evaporated.

Myron looked at his fingernails. They had an unusual yellow cast that he had not noticed before. The sparse hair on his arms looked yellow, too, and felt slick, as if he'd been rubbing hair tonic into it.

"What's going on?" Princess asked. Her voice shook a little, and Myron didn't blame her. Something terrible was happening to their bodies.

"You're turning into P'yugch People," Marsy Batter said.

"What?" Myron and Princess cried together. At last the condition they had seen when the dandelion mush exploded had a name.

"The P'yugch People are former enemies of mine who were less successful than Lupoff, and Trayne, and Ted. One by one, singly and in bunches, I caught them and their armies and kept them in one of my pumpkins until they changed. The same thing is happening to you."

Myron didn't know what to say. But the idea of turning into one of those horrible unbaked creatures—to have no mind of his own, to act entirely at the whim of Marsy Batter—was the most awful thing he could think of. Here was another fate worse than a quick, clean death.

"The process began when you entered the pumpkin," Marsy Batter explained. "Until you change to p'yugch entirely, the process can be reversed by leaving the pumpkin. But you will not leave until I am satisfied that *I* know all *you* know. I hope we understand each other."

"But comic books *aren't real*," Myron cried. "Everything in them is made up."

"Then you will become a permanent P'yugch Person."

"What about me?" Princess asked.

"You will be taken to the graylands and left there."

"You can't do that," Myron said. "She's my assistant. I can't build a thing without her."

"Your *huh?*" Princess said.

While Marsy Batter studied them, Myron was aware that with each passing second more of him was becoming p'yugch. "Very well," she said. "To the laboratory."

Her ring shot light all around as she hustled them across the room. She pushed through a beaded curtain and into a room almost as large as the main hall they'd encountered first. It contained large tables—some of which had controls and readout screens built in, tall structures as big around as houses, and a thing that might have been either a weapon or a telescope angled down from the ceiling. P'yugch hung from everything like moss.

"Remember," Marsy Batter said, "the faster you work, the better your chances of getting out of this in your original forms."

The speed at which Myron worked wouldn't matter. Anything he did he would just be making up as he went. "Right," he said. "Could we get something to eat? We're starved." Myron figured he had an even chance of getting fed. After all, he and Princess couldn't do their best work if they were hungry.

"Perhaps after you produce a weapon or two I will consider it," Marsy Batter said, and went back through the beaded curtain.

As soon as she was gone, Myron and Princess began to prowl, looking for a way out of the laboratory and perhaps out of the pumpkin. No exit immediately presented itself. Even the beaded curtain, which looked so promising, would not part for them; it was as solid as a stone wall.

Myron climbed onto the big sink against the wall and looked out a window. What he saw pleased him. He climbed down from the sink and nodded at Princess. They turned on every machine they could find. Soon the air was filled with buzzing and thumping and whirring. Altogether, the noises made quite a racket. Now Myron and Princess could talk without fear of being overheard.

"The graylands are just outside," Myron whispered. "This laboratory must be right on the shell."

"Down here in the depths of the pumpkin?" Princess exclaimed. "I guess the space inside the pumpkin must be twisted in some funny ways."

"I guess. But thank goodness. Being next to the shell makes our job easier."

Princess pondered that for a moment. "You claimed I was your assistant so Marsy Batter wouldn't pitch me out into the graylands alone, and now you want us to escape out there together?"

"No, listen to me," Myron said eagerly. Princess seemed doubtful as Myron laid out his plan. When he was done, he watched her for some sign of approval.

"You're asking an awful lot of coincidence," Princess said.

"Ordinarily, I'd agree with you," Myron said, "but the ghosts we saw convince me that we'll get home all right. We already have the disease. Look." He held up his hands to show her that they had become bloated and yellow—not as bloated and yellow as they would be, but the process had definitely begun. "And our hair is turning to p'yugch."

Princess pulled a strand of her bangs down, and she stared at it cross-eyed.

"The dandelion mush explosion allowed us to see ourselves in the future. We were obviously standing in the clearing where A.L. planted his pumpkin seed, which makes sense—that's where this pumpkin is going.

That had to be a time shortly after we escaped from the pumpkin because we were still p'yugchy."

"The dandelion the ghost-Myron was pointing to fits in," Princess admitted.

"Right. What do you think?"

"I think it's weird. We know we'll escape, but we don't know how." Princess shook her head. "All right. Go for it. I don't look good in p'yugch."

They turned off the machines and called for Marsy Batter. She showed up a moment later, evidence that she or one of her P'yugch People had been listening.

"We need dandelions," Myron told her.

"For what purpose?" Marsy Batter seemed suspicious.

"You want weapons, we need dandelions," Myron said.

"Very well," Marsy Batter replied. "But if this is a trick, I will inject you both with pumpkin juice. You will become P'yugch People instantly."

Marsy Batter's threat didn't bother Myron

much because he knew that tricking her was his only chance. He and Princess followed Marsy Batter across the room, but she stopped before she reached the beaded curtain and turned on them suddenly.

"Where do you think you're going?" she asked.

"Picking dandelions," Princess reminded her.

"I did not sprout with the last rain," Marsy Batter explained. "My P'yugch People will pick dandelions. You wait here. Is a bushel enough?"

Myron considered Marsy Batter's question and was torn. The more dandelions he had, the better. Yet he didn't want the P'yugch People to take any more time than necessary. The p'yugch was running strong in his body. "Yes," he said. "A bushel is enough." How much was a bushel, anyway?

Marsy Batter nodded and left.

They sat down at a laboratory bench but did not wait long before a P'yugch Person staggered into the room carrying a basket the size of a washtub. It was full of dandelions.

The P'yugch Person moved woodenly, but for a second Myron thought he saw some intelligence in its eyes, some suggestion of long and almost unbearable suffering. Myron moved to get a better look, but when he positioned himself properly, whatever intelligence he might have seen in its eyes was gone. They held no more feeling than the eyes of a jack-o'-lantern.

Myron watched with dread as the P'yugch Person set the basket down on the laboratory table. In a short time, he and Princess could be P'yugch People. Seeing the P'yugch Person up close and personal made Myron even more determined to escape, no matter what the cost.

The bushel basket full of dandelions was too big to fit into the microp'yugch oven. (That's what the badge on the front said it was—an All Hallows Microp'yugch Oven.) So he and Princess lifted handfuls and stuffed them inside. By the time they were finished, the microp'yugch oven held a solid brick of dandelions, from top to bottom and from side to side.

Princess closed the oven door. "Do you really think this will work?" she asked.

"We got out of here somehow," Myron said. "We saw ourselves in the clearing like this." He held up his hands. They were more yellow than ever, and the bloating had made its way a small but perceptible distance up his wrists. Soon he'd look like Popeye. If his plan didn't work, he and Princess might not have a second chance.

"That doesn't answer my question," Princess said.

He shrugged. "You know as much as I do. Are you ready?"

"Push the button," Princess said.

Myron programmed the microp'yugch to run for nine hours and sixty minutes. He was sure that was too long—maybe five or ten minutes would be sufficient—but he would rather the cycle go on too long than stop too soon. The dandelions needed enough energy to explode. After that the microp'yugch would likely stop by itself. He took a deep breath and punched the Start button.

He joined Princess where she crouched behind a lab bench.

The waiting was awful. Myron wanted to peek out from behind the bench, but he knew that was not only dangerous but ridiculous. Watching the digital timer count down would not make the explosion come sooner.

Since Uncle Hugo had begun his experiments with dandelions, Myron's whole life seemed to be marked by a series of explosions. First the dandelion mush, then the black boink, and now—if he was lucky—the dandelions in the microp'yugch oven.

"This isn't going to work," Princess said. "A microp'yugch oven is no atomic furnace."

"Neither is a wood fire," Myron reminded her. He thought of that day (Yesterday? Tomorrow? Who knew?) in the barn when the dandelion mush had exploded. Life had seemed a lot simpler then.

Myron was about to give in to his urge to have a look when suddenly the loudest noise he'd ever heard blew past him, causing him to curl up tight against Princess and the bench. It was a boom that shook everything in the kitchen, including the teeth in his head. Black smoke billowed around them, making them cough and their eyes water.

TIME LEAP IV

A TORNADO PICKS UP THE BOY AND THE GIRL AND THE BLOND MAN IN THE COVERALLS.

IT WHIRLS THEM AROUND, CAUSING THEM TO BARELY MISS DINOSAURS, KNIGHTS IN ARMOR, ANTIGRAVITY CARS, AND A GIANT HAND WEARING A PUMPKIN-SHAPED CRYSTAL RING.

HAND OVER HAND, THE MAN IN THE COVERALLS SWIMS THROUGH THE MESS TOWARD THE BOY. WHILE TRYING TO AVOID THE MAN, THE BOY IS NEARLY GRABBED BY THE HUGE HAND.

11 WEEDABATER

Blinking and coughing against the smoke, Myron and Princess looked out from behind the bench and saw that the microp'yugch oven was gone. Most of the counter it had been sitting on was gone, too. A big ragged hole had been punched through the pumpkin wall; the edges still smoked where they glowed orange. So much smoke poured out the hole that Myron could not see what was outside, but the smoke seemed to glow a little, as if light was filtering through it. The sun was probably up.

He took Princess's hand, and together they ran through the hole. Myron gulped the fresh air down as if it were cool water. He was relieved that he'd been right about the future. Of course, all bets were off now. Anything could happen. There were no more glimpses into the future—no more guarantees.

The air cleared a little, and he saw that he was indeed in the clearing where A.L. had planted the pumpkin—Myron recognized the shark cherub. It made sense. After all, according to Marsy Batter, the pumpkin they'd been riding in was the same one A.L. had planted. If it was here in their present, the pumpkin must be ripe. Myron squinted up at the sun. It seemed to be late afternoon, but of what day?

"Come on," Myron said. "Marsy Batter should be sending P'yugch People to investigate any minute." He ran toward the trees but stopped when Princess pointed.

"Look," she said.

Myron looked where Princess was pointing and saw ghostly images of the two of them and Uncle Hugo floating in the air along with many globs of dandelion mush and splinters of an exploded vat. Behind them, he could see the faint details of the barn. It had to be the three of them in the past, back before they knew anything about A.L. or pumpkins or Marsy Batter. The circle was closed.

Myron needed to tell the earlier versions of themselves that as bad as things might get, everything would turn out all right. He searched through his pockets for a dandelion. Though the p'yugch swelling seemed to have gone down a little, the search was made difficult by the fact that his hands were still about twice their normal size and the joints did not work properly. However, he found the dandelion and pointed to it madly.

"Use the exploding dandelions in the microp'yugch oven to escape from Marsy Batter!" he cried, though he knew the earlier

Myron and Princess could neither hear nor understand. He and the current Princess certainly hadn't. He was about to try another message, but the earlier scene disappeared as suddenly as if a door had been slammed between their two times.

They heard the sounds of many people moving clumsily around the lab inside the big pumpkin. Without further discussion, Myron and Princess ran in among the trees. Myron doubted their ability to avoid the P'yugch People for long.

"We need to stop Marsy Batter," Princess said, "but I don't want to go back inside the pumpkin if I don't have to."

"Maybe there's another way," Myron said. He still occasionally coughed up smoke. Between his need for more oxygen, the appearance of the ghostly vision of his past, and the sudden pursuit by the P'yugch People, his head spun. "I need time to think," he said without hope of getting it. The P'yugch People entered the forest and crashed through the undergrowth.

THE TORNADO GRADUALLY
DIES AWAY, DEPOSITING THE BOY, THE GIRL,
AND THE MAN ON THE GROUND—AND
LEAVING THE SURROUNDING FOREST
DRAPED IN PUMPKIN P'YUGCH.

IN ANOTHER PART OF THE FOREST,
A SIMILAR BOY AND A SIMILAR GIRL TAKE
TURNS CARRYING A HEAVY RED CYLINDER
AS THEY RUN, THEY ARE PURSUED
BY A SIMILAR MAN AND AN ARMY OF
THOUSANDS OF PEOPLE WHO LOOK AS IF
THEY'D BEEN CARVED OUT OF PUMPKIN
MEAT BY A THREE-YEAR-OLD.

"THE MYRON,"
THE PUMPKIN PEOPLE MOAN.
"THE MYRON."

"They're moving a lot faster than I expected," Princess said.

"Yeah," Myron said. "It looks as if Marsy Batter has come up with a new improved P'yugch Person."

"P'yugch Person version two-point-zero," Princess suggested.

"It doesn't matter what version they are," he said. "They're still p'yugch—you know, vegetable people. And maybe that's their weakness."

"You have another plan?" Princess asked as she trotted along behind him. She sounded breathless, and the truth was that Myron was not in such hot shape either. Being part p'yugch didn't help, even if the p'yugch was clearing up like a bad rash.

"I'll show you everything when we get there," Myron said as he stomped along.

They concentrated on moving fast and did not speak again until they reached the mansion. The sounds of the P'yugch People stumbling through the forest had faded in the distance, but they were obviously still on the trail.

"Uncle Hugo!" Myron cried out. An extra hand would be useful right now. "Uncle Hugo!"

"Where is he?" Princess asked.

"Assuming it's the same day we left, he's probably still at his meeting at Astronetics. He's trying to sell them on his theories of food preservation."

They ran to the far side of the mansion, where Myron entered a small wooden shed. Princess stood next to him looking down at the gardening tools, empty flowerpots, bags of fertilizer, and lawn mowers.

"What are we searching for?" Princess asked. Worriedly, she peered out the door of the shed.

Myron moved a bag of fertilizer. "This," he said as he hauled a red cylinder outside. It stood on three small legs. On top was a pump handle, and a thin hose hung from one side. "This is a Weedabater," Myron explained. "Hugo keeps it around to kill weeds."

"Not very organic," Princess said with disapproval.

"Maybe not, but it works. I want to spray around the pumpkin. You've seen what a Halloween pumpkin looks like if you keep it too long? If we play our cards right, the Weedabater should make Marsy Batter's pumpkin collapse just like a month-old jack-o'-lantern."

Myron was shocked to see an army of P'yugch People emerge quickly from the forest, calling his name. They were neither beautiful nor graceful, but they moved a lot faster than the P'yugch People he had seen inside the pumpkin.

"Let's shoot them already if we're going to," Princess cried.

"We can't hit them from this range. They'll have to come closer."

"Don't shoot till you see the orange of their eyes," Princess said.

And indeed, the P'yugch People were approaching quickly.

"The Myron. The Myron."

Myron gripped the pump handle and

Princess aimed the nozzle of the hose at the front rank of P'yugch People. Myron watched anxiously as they got closer. He waited as long as he dared, then he pumped the handle with a vigorous up-and-down motion. Soon, a heavy spray of Weedabater struck them.

Myron felt a keen satisfaction when the leading P'yugch People began to smoke, turn black, and curl in on themselves. The P'yugch People who'd been hit stopped walking but otherwise seemed unbothered by what was happening to them. The blank stares never left their unfinished faces as they crumpled to the ground, which was just as well. If Myron had seen any intelligence in their eyes, as he had in the eyes of the P'yugch Person who delivered the dandelions, he could not have continued.

A few seconds later, all of the lead P'yugch People were nothing more than ashes that blew away in the light breeze.

Myron kept pumping.

Oblivious to what had happened to their

comrades, the rest of the P'yugch People continued to advance. As they came into range, Princess played the Weedabater up and back across them. They all curled into black ash, too, and blew away.

Myron supposed that not even Marsy Batter could have unlimited enemies to turn into P'yugch People, but such a crowd continued to attack that Myron worried that he would run out of Weedabater before he'd destroyed them all—or even worse, before he had a chance to spray Marsy Batter's pumpkin.

Marsy Batter herself stepped out of the woods then, surprising Myron so much that he stopped spraying for a moment. She stood there calmly, her ring flashing at her side in the slanting sunlight. "Now, you will deal with me," Marsy Batter said.

12 LOOP
THE
LOOP

"Marsy Batter grew in a pod," Myron whispered to Princess. "She's a vegetable person, just like the P'yugch People."

"Gotcha," Princess said.

"All right," Myron called to Marsy Batter. "You win." When he stepped forward, two P'yugch People grabbed him roughly and half-dragged him toward the edge of the forest. Marsy Batter watched him intently as he approached.

The two P'yugch People stood him in front of Marsy Batter while the others stopped where they were and waited without showing a sign of interest.

"One way or another, O Myron, you will not escape again," Marsy Batter said.

Myron's heart was beating fast. "Maybe I won't have to," he said as calmly as he could. Out of the tip of his eye he could see that Princess had moved in close enough. "Now!" he cried.

The Weedabater spray struck Marsy Batter in the chest and her eyes opened as if she'd been doused in cold water. "I'm melting," she remarked calmly, as if she was analyzing a new but only mildly interesting experience. "Melting."

Princess continued to spray her blackening form.

"I'll be back!" Marsy Batter suddenly cried in a louder voice than Myron had ever heard her use. She crumpled into ash, and Princess started spraying the remaining P'yugch People.

Myron was able to shrug himself out of

the grasp of the two holding him, and he ran back to Princess. He took over pumping the Weedabater handle while she held the nozzle steady; they made sure that nothing was left of Marsy Batter.

A.L. emerged from the forest near what was left of Marsy Batter, tossing a time bomb boink in one hand. "What are you kids doing?" he called.

"That must be a trick question," Myron grumbled to Princess.

The shortest way back to the pumpkin was right past A.L., but taking that route obviously wasn't possible. Myron picked up the cylinder and, cradling it as if it were a baby, ran into the forest some distance from him. Myron's plan was to circle around A.L. and then head straight for the pumpkin.

Princess was right behind Myron. And right behind Princess, Myron feared, were A.L. and the five or six remaining P'yugch People. Somewhere nearby, he heard an explosion.

Not again, he thought.

Myron tingled all over. He moved very slowly, which was too bad because the Weedabater cylinder seemed as heavy as ever. Near him Princess left a trail of rainbows as she pumped through the air, which was suddenly gluey and thick. He heard no sound but a loud rushing, as of wind through an ancient forest.

Obviously A.L. had hurled a time bomb boink at them, but they were just out of range. The blast affected them, but it had been too far away to pitch them into the graylands between universal cars.

Myron concentrated on running as quickly as he could, which was not very fast.

Suddenly everything was normal again. He kept running as he glanced over his shoulder and saw that the bomb had carved out a small crater. A circle of trees was missing, certainly blown into the graylands. Myron wondered if they could live there or if they would eventually starve, just as people would.

Myron gave the cylinder to Princess and

shook his hands to restore their circulation. She didn't say anything but hunched over the cylinder and continued running.

Another time bomb boink exploded behind them. It seemed to Myron that this time the rainbows were drawn-out, the rushing louder, the entire effect much stronger. A.L. was catching up. The next time he threw a boink, it would explode close enough to send them into the graylands. And if A.L. didn't get them, the P'yugch People would.

They arrived at the pumpkin, and Princess put down the cylinder.

"All right, Myron," Princess said breathlessly, "now that we're here, why are we here?"

"To Weedabate the pumpkin, remember?" He pulled up on the cylinder's pump handle.

"But Marsy Batter is dead. We liquidated her."

"She said she'd be back."

"You believe her?"

"*I* don't want to take a chance that pumpkin will grow another Marsy Batter, do *you?*"

Princess picked up the hose and aimed the nozzle at the pumpkin. "Fire when ready," she said.

Behind them A.L. ran into the clearing. He saw them, but before he could throw another time bomb boink, two more people ran into the clearing from the other side. Myron was so astonished to see who they were that even the thought of his own destruction was pushed aside. A.L. seemed to be astonished, too, because he stared at the newcomers, his arm cocked and the black boink forgotten.

Though the two new people were covered from head to foot with pumpkin p'yugch, it was obvious that they were Myron and A.L. Where was Princess?

The p'yugch-covered A.L. and the p'yugch-covered Myron waved their arms above their heads as if the road was closed ahead.

"Stop!" the p'yugch-covered Myron shouted. "Don't use the Weedabater on the pumpkin!"

The p'yugch-covered A.L. shouted the

same message now, as both he and the p'yugch-covered Myron continued to wave their arms.

"I don't know who that is," Myron said, "but if he's with A.L., I don't trust him."

"They might be P'yugch People," Princess agreed. She began to pump the cylinder, spraying the Weedabater all over the pumpkin. The trunklike stem that anchored the pumpkin to the ground started to smoke.

"Yikes!" the p'yugch-covered Myron cried. He and the p'yugch-covered A.L. ran back into the forest.

"Keep spraying," Myron ordered Princess. He turned and saw A.L. still paralyzed in throwing position by what he had seen. Where were the P'yugch People? Myron wondered. They should have arrived by now.

Myron ran at A.L. and tackled him. A.L. squished when he hit the ground. While fighting to avoid inhaling the fishy smell, Myron was able to wrestle the black boink from A.L.'s hand and toss it into the bushes. A good thing A.L. had not yet pulled the stem.

He looked back just as Marsy Batter's pumpkin began to unravel. Even counting his recent experiences, Myron had never seen anything so strange. A thread of pumpkin rose into the sky like smoke. The thread spun itself out longer and longer, taking more and more of the pumpkin, kicking up wind that became stronger as the thread lengthened into an enormous tornado.

Myron was terrified to find himself sucked into the tornado and whirled into the sky along with Princess, A.L., and everything else that was not tied down. Wind blew around him in a single strong gust that went on and on, causing dust and strands of unraveled pumpkin to strike him. The strands soon hardened into p'yugch.

He was shocked further to see other stuff whirling around, too: a triceratops, a stegosaur, a guy dressed in armor, and a futuristic vehicle. They must all be caught in some kind of time vortex!

Then an enormous hand—each finger as

big as Myron—reached out from the center of the vortex and made a few grabs at him. Swimming as best he could through the rough air, Myron managed to maneuver out of its way but almost flew into A.L.'s arms! Being accosted by a giant hand was bad enough, but making it worse was that one finger wore a crystal pumpkin ring, just like Marsy Batter's.

The giant hand gave Myron lots to think about before the time vortex blew itself out and slowly lowered him back to the ground. The giant hand confused and frightened him. He and Princess had destroyed Marsy Batter, and now here she was back again, only bigger. Was the one they'd destroyed the same one they'd seen on A.L.'s screen? Was the one on the screen the same one they'd seen in the pod? How many were there? And how *big* were they? Confusion threatened to overwhelm him, but he wouldn't let it. Though the prospect depressed him, he'd take his Marsy Batters as they came.

Once on the ground, he shook p'yugch

from his hands and tried to scrape the worst of it from his face and clothing. Getting clean would be impossible without a shower and a change of clothes. P'yugch was in his hair and down inside his shirt. He was not only slimy, he smelled even more like a pumpkin than he had when he was turning into a P'yugch Person.

A.L. and Princess sat nearby, as dirty as he was and obviously as dazed. Through the entire storm Princess had kept her hold on the Weedabater. It lay beside her. Myron could not see dinosaurs, air cars, men in armor, or giant hands with flashy rings. He hoped they each had been whirled back to their own time.

"I was supposed to send you to the future in that pumpkin," A.L. said to Myron furiously, "and now it's gone." A.L. took another black boink from his bandoleer, and he began to toss it. "You kids ruined me," he went on, "and now I'm going to ruin you." The thought of ruining them made him chuckle.

Myron was fascinated by the boink, but it didn't bother him as much as it had before. He'd survived worse threats. A.L. was no doubt dangerous, but Myron didn't have to curl up and blow away.

"Marsy Batter is the one who let us escape," Princess said. "She can't blame her own failure on you. Besides, she can't blame anybody for anything anymore."

"Marsy Batter can do anything she wants," A.L. assured her. "Even now."

"Then you'd better watch where you toss that black sphere," Myron said. "Marsy Batter won't want me harmed."

A.L. continued to toss his boink thoughtfully. Occasionally he giggled, sounding like a loose bolt in a hubcap.

Myron found it annoying. "I've had about enough of A.L.'s psychotic snickers," he said to Princess. He stood up and glanced around.

"Psychotic Snickers—isn't that an insane candy bar?" Princess said, obviously pleased with herself.

"Come on," Myron said. "Let's see if Uncle Hugo is back."

"Wait a minute," Princess said. She shook her head to clear it. "When are we?"

"*When* are we?" Myron asked, mystified.

Myron heard explosions from the other side of Hugo's property.

"Sounds like time bomb boinks," Princess said. "The time vortex must have sent us back in time a few minutes."

"A.L. throws a lot of time bomb boinks," Myron reminded her.

A.L. giggled.

"Yes, but the only occasion he threw one after another like that was when he was chasing us through the forest."

Myron was fascinated by Princess's idea. If it was true, *another* A.L. and the remains of Marsy Batter's P'yugch-Person army were chasing *another* Myron and *another* Princess (all three of them much cleaner than he was, Myron thought ruefully) through the forest, heaving time bomb boinks at them. They had not yet Weedabated the big pumpkin.

Myron tried to get his mind around the situation. He longed for a piece of paper and pencil so he could make a diagram, but as best he could figure it, they were in a time loop: the explosion of the pumpkin caused the time road to detour back in time instead of going straight, so that it circled around and crossed itself, forcing the universal car to travel through the same moment again before it went on.

A.L. slowly rose to his feet, making martial arts passes through the air with his hands. "*Kreega!*" he suddenly cried. "If we really are a few minutes in the past, we have a chance to stop your earlier selves from blowing up the pumpkin."

"Why would we want to do that?" Princess asked.

"The Marsy Batter you met in the pumpkin was just an advanced kind of P'yugch Person. The real Marsy Batter grows them and sends them out on these little missions."

Myron had a sinking feeling. "*Real* Marsy Batter?" he asked.

"Yes," A.L. went on. "If you destroy her pumpkin, she herself will come to see what's wrong. I guarantee that none of us will like that. Let's get a move on. Our earlier selves will be here in a minute." He shoved the boink back into his bandoleer.

Princess pulled Myron aside. "What do you think?" she asked.

"Maybe A.L.'s telling the truth. The giant hand in the time vortex was wearing Marsy Batter's ring."

"So, is Marsy Batter a giant or did the time vortex magnify her hand somehow?"

"Does it matter?" Myron asked. "I say we take a chance on A.L. this once. I don't want to see Marsy Batter again, do you?"

"Trusting soul," Princess said. "All right. Let's do it."

He remembered that when their earlier selves had arrived at the pumpkin, he'd wondered what had happened to the P'yugch People. Now he knew. "Princess, take that Weedabater and dissolve the P'yugch People chasing our earlier selves."

Myron could see that Princess was inclined to give him an argument, but she didn't. "Right," was all she said, then hurried away lugging the Weedabater cylinder.

Myron and A.L. ran for the clearing.

Having A.L. on their side was odd. Myron knew he was helping them protect the pumpkin only because he had failed and they had succeeded. No doubt A.L. still hoped to save his own hide by sending Myron to the future.

Myron was the first to reach the pumpkin. The clean Myron and the clean Princess—they were orange and stringy, but they weren't actually covered in anything—were already there, preparing to douse it with Weedabater. A clean A.L. was about to fling a time bomb boink at them, but he stopped, paralyzed by surprise when he saw the p'yugch-covered Myron and A.L. emerge from the forest waving their arms above their heads.

"Stop!" Myron shouted. "Don't use the Weedabater on the pumpkin!" He waved his arms, though he remembered his own dark suspicions when he saw two p'yugch-covered individuals enter the clearing, and he knew his efforts were in vain.

"Stop," A.L. cried.

The earlier Myron and Princess spoke

briefly. She began to pump the cylinder, spraying the Weedabater at the pumpkin. The trunklike stem that anchored the pumpkin to the ground started to smoke.

"Yikes!" the later Myron cried. He and A.L. ran back into the forest, where Myron collided with someone running the other way. It was Princess, of course. *His* Princess. She'd left the Weedabater cylinder somewhere. It was certainly empty by now.

"We can't stay here," Myron cried. "That pumpkin's about to unravel into a time vortex. It could blow us into next week."

The pumpkin unraveled again for the first time. When it did, Myron had a strange experience—not as strange as when the time mush exploded, but definitely outside his normal realm. He could see the time vortex spinning over the forest—carrying people and things, throwing off pumpkin threads, thrashing the trees—and yet he felt no wind himself. It was almost like watching a movie, but far stranger because he was right there and feeling nothing.

The time vortex gradually died down and left the trees alone, though slimy strings and webs of p'yugch now hung from their branches. The intense smell of fresh pumpkin that filled the forest made Myron's nose itch.

Once more he tried to understand the time loop. The Myron and Princess and A.L. he'd tried to prevent from blowing up the pumpkin were now a few minutes in the past trying to prevent *another* set of Myron and Princess and A.L. from blowing up the pumpkin— an action that the present Myron knew would not work. Meanwhile, yet *another* Myron- and-Princess team, heading for the pumpkin with a cylinder of Weedabater, were being chased through the forest by their own A.L. and their own group of P'yugch People. The third Myron and Princess would refuse to listen to the second batch.

He imagined an infinite conga line of My- rons, Princesses, A.L.s, and P'yugch People, each individual working his or her way through the loop and then moving on into the future. Myron shook his head as his mind boggled. The picture would make a great comic book cover if anybody could master the perspective of the situation.

Whatever happened next to him and the other people in his batch would actually happen next for the first time—at least for them—which was refreshing, considering their adventures with time mush, time bomb boinks, graylands, and the time vortex.

"Thinking four-dimensionally is a bear," Myron said.

"Don't do it," Princess advised him. She looked around anxiously. "Where's A.L.?" she asked.

"Hiding from the vortex, I suppose," Myron said. He pulled some slime off his chest and threw it at the ground. "I need a shower," he said. Now that the excitement was over, he felt he deserved it.

For the moment the only difficulty left to overcome was the presence of A.L. Maybe now that Marsy Batter and her pumpkin were gone—twice?!—A.L. could be convinced to just get into his truck and leave before the *real* Marsy Batter arrived, if she actually existed. Such a solution seemed too easy. More likely, A.L. was preparing to spring something on them. If he had merely gone into hiding from the second explosion, he should have emerged long since.

"I could use a shower, too," Princess said. "But will we have a chance? I have the feeling that the truce with A.L. is over."

"I agree. What about the *real* Marsy Batter?"

"You're still thinking about the giant hand, aren't you?"

"Wouldn't you if you were me?"

"Maybe your uncle Hugo can help," Princess said.

"We've done all right by ourselves so far," Myron reminded her.

"We have," Princess said, "but I'm pretty much out of ideas."

"It's true," Myron agreed. "A fresh outlook couldn't hurt."

They set off for the barn. As they walked, Myron had an opportunity to think about their adventures instead of just dealing with them. Something seemed not quite right. "Did you notice something interesting when the dandelions blew up Marsy Batter's lab?" Myron asked.

"Just your average garden-variety temporal explosion," Princess said.

"That's just it," Myron said excitedly. "It wasn't temporal." He remembered the rainbows and the noise and the prickly electricity when the dandelion mush had exploded in the barn. In the pumpkin none of that had happened.

Princess seemed stunned by Myron's statement. "You're right," she cried. "No rainbows! But it *had* to be a temporal explosion—we used dandelions."

"Then there's obviously something else going on," Myron said. He could not help wondering whether the use of the microp'yugch oven had anything to do with the lack of rainbows. But energy was energy, wasn't it, whether you applied it with microp'yugch or with burning wood? He pondered the circumstances surrounding the explosion and suddenly he knew the answer.

"It's the pumpkin meat," Myron said.

"What's the pumpkin meat?"

"The reason we didn't see rainbows. Anything made of pumpkin must be immune. Everything in Marsy Batter's kitchen was made of pumpkin—including us. Maybe that's why they travel through time in pumpkins, because it insulates them somehow; the shell keeps the time outside separate from the time inside."

"Wow," Princess exclaimed. She frowned. "But if that's true," she said, "when A.L. was chasing us through the forest his time bomb boinks should have had no effect on us. And neither should the unraveling of the pumpkin. We were still part p'yugch."

Princess was right. Their nails and hair were still yellow, as they had been in Marsy Batter's living room. Even so, he and Princess were a lot less p'yugchy than they had been. Obviously once they left the pumpkin they'd begun to change back, and the process had gone on long enough that they were once again affected by temporal explosions, not just physical ones. Myron told Princess his theory.

She nodded and agreed that it made sense, given the evidence.

They arrived at the barn safely and found it to be full of p'yugch, no doubt blown in there by the time vortex. A new vat of dandelions bubbled gently over a fire, filling the barn with the green smell. H.G. Wells was sleeping curled up on Princess's sorting table.

"No Hugo," Princess said.

"Let's check the mansion. I'd welcome a little adult supervision right now."

"Well, now, look at this," someone said. It was A.L. without his disguise. He was standing in the doorway chuckling and holding a ring-flinger pistol with one tentacle so it was aimed at Myron.

13 WAR AND P'YUGCH

A.L. looked like a malign squid and smelled like a dead fish, but he was no longer covered in p'yugch. Myron guessed that he'd taken off the unraveled pumpkin along with his disguise.

"We were wondering what happened to you," Princess said coolly.

"I've been planting another pumpkin to take Myron to the future in," A.L. said. "That was the scheme all along, though

Marsy Batter was supposed to do the taking."

"I explained to Marsy Batter about comic books," Myron said. "They're not real. Those weapons don't exist."

"One of them exists now," A.L. said proudly. He motioned with his ring-flinger. "I built it myself."

Myron didn't know whether to laugh or to cry. The proper response depended a lot on whether A.L.'s weapon worked as well as the one the pig used in the comic book. If A.L. was as ignorant of comic book physics as Marsy Batter, maybe it didn't. Myron was afraid to be the one who would find out for sure, but he didn't want Princess or H.G. hurt, either. His indecision froze him.

"If you want a free demonstration," A.L. said as he grinned at Myron, "just refuse to come to my truck."

"What's there?" Myron asked.

"Job security for me. I want you in a safe place till tomorrow when the new pumpkin is ripe. I don't want to be a P'yugch Person. Understand?"

It struck Myron that he'd like A.L. better

as a P'yugch Person. He'd be easier to manage, anyway. For now Myron would just have to distract A.L. with conversation until he had time to think up a plan.

"I thought all you guys from the future travel in pumpkins," Myron said. "How come you use a truck?"

"I'm not from the future," A.L. said. "My truck is a space vehicle, not a time machine. I'm Marsy Batter's local—local in time, anyway—agent." A.L. waved the ring-flinger. "Come on, Myron," he said.

H.G. meowed, and they all looked at her. She was sitting on the table yawning widely.

"Fur ball," A.L. said with delight. He raised his weapon.

Suddenly Myron knew what to do—and it needed to be done immediately. It was so dangerous that if he thought about it, he wouldn't do it. Myron did it.

At the same instant, A.L. fired and Myron dropped behind the vat to scoop up a double handful of p'yugch from the floor; he hurled it at A.L.—it struck him full in the face with a splat. A.L. took a wild shot and concentric rings struck the table near H.G. She leapt away as the table glowed brighter and brighter and then exploded into sparks.

"Great Frooth!" Princess cried. "It works!"

Myron threw another handful of p'yugch. It struck A.L.'s weapon and knocked it from his hand. He felt anger and fear, but there were no further plans in his head, no thoughts at all.

Princess quickly picked her way across the slick floor. She grabbed the ring-flinger before A.L. had a chance to clear the p'yugch from his eyes and then retreated to a corner, from which she aimed the weapon at him.

Now that he allowed himself to think, Myron was terrified by the brave things he and Princess had just done. They could not have stopped A.L. any more smoothly if they'd had one of those power gloves they'd seen in the comics. Seemingly unbothered by the wet, icky p'yugch, H.G. sat down at Myron's feet and began to wash.

H.G. was obviously more than just a cat. Both A.L. and Marsy Batter believed she was worth worrying about, and though H.G. had not done anything a normal cat wouldn't do, she *had* meowed at just the right moment. When this was all over, he and Princess and Uncle Hugo would have to find out more about her.

A.L. carefully picked great webs of p'yugch off his face, but he made no threatening move. He seemed to be entirely whipped, though Myron did not trust appearances. Even covered by the flinger, A.L. was still dangerous. Myron took up a handful of warm p'yugch and held it ready to throw. H.G. purred.

"You kids and that fur ball are a lot of trouble," A.L. grumbled. Like a magician he produced a handkerchief from somewhere behind his back, and as they conversed wiped every bit of p'yugch off his face.

Myron saw that he *could* talk his way out of this after all. He shook his head at how easy it would be, at how dumb they had all been not to see it immediately. "You still don't get it," he said. "The weapon *works*. That should be worth something to Marsy Batter. If you can build *one* comic book weapon that works, why can't you build others?"

A.L. was so stunned, he actually stopped grooming for a moment. Evidently the idea that he could be a satisfactory replacement for The Myron had not occurred to him. At last he nodded. "You're right," he said. "I'll use the flinger as a sample when I get to the future. Hand it over."

"Surely you jest," Princess said.

Another standoff, Myron thought with despair. A.L. seemed to be friendly again, but his sunny disposition might evaporate once he had what he wanted. And he might abduct Myron, too, as insurance.

On the other hand, it was unlikely that A.L. would leave without his weapon.

Myron didn't know what to do. They couldn't stand there forever trading quips. He glanced at H.G., hoping she might do some perfect catlike thing, but she just sat with her feet tucked under her. Suddenly the air in the middle of the room seemed to thicken. Then it began to spin as if somebody was stirring it.

Myron stared at the moving air with surprise, thinking it looked a lot like a time vortex; indeed, Myron again had the strange sensation of seeing wind around him without feeling it. The air spun faster and faster and began to pick up dirt and p'yugch and dandelion mush.

The vortex exploded (*Another* explosion! thought Myron), and with a roar a huge pumpkin burst into the room from nowhere. H.G. leapt into Myron's arms as he ducked behind the vat. The pumpkin knocked furniture aside and blew out planks from the barn's walls and roof.

Myron doubted whether the creature or thing that emerged from the pumpkin would regard a handful of pumpkin p'yugch as a weapon. Princess had the ring-flinger, of course, and that might be helpful. He was amazed at how calm he was, though he wondered if his self-possession was a sign of stu-pidity.

A section of pumpkin shell separated itself from the rest of the wall, and then it moved aside to reveal a p'yugch curtain. A hand pushed the curtain aside. It was a normal-size hand, but as the arm and then the body followed, everything unfolded in a direction that—as it seemed to Myron—slid off his eyes.

Princess gave a little *yip!*

If the roof of the barn hadn't been blown off by the pumpkin's arrival, Marsy Batter would have burst through it now. Estimating how tall she had grown was difficult, but it was many stories. She now matched the enor-mous hand Myron had seen in the time vor-tex, even to the crystal pumpkin ring. She waved around a pistol with knobs and nurdles and flashing lights on it, but the armament wasn't necessary.

Myron gulped as he looked up at her. She was like the Statue of Liberty come alive and gone mean.

Marsy Batter raised her arms. "People of Earth!" she cried in a booming voice that must have been heard in the next county. "I am Marsy Batter, and I have come for what is mine!"

14 GONE WITH THE P'YUGCH

This woman had not grown on any stem. Whatever cold intelligence the fake Marsy Batter had radiated was nothing compared with the bad vibes given off by the real Marsy Batter. Just standing next to her frightened Myron, and not only because she might step on him by accident.

A.L. had warned them the real Marsy Batter might show up if her pumpkin was destroyed, and here she was. A.L. hadn't lied about that, anyway. Too bad.

"Oh, the shy type," Princess commented under her breath.

Marsy Batter brought her weapon around to point it at Princess. Princess seemed to be staring up the barrel of a cannon. Marsy Batter gazed at her mildly, in total control, and Myron was afraid that something terrible was about to happen. He was actually relieved when Marsy Batter aimed the weapon at each of them, including A.L. and H.G., in turn.

"You were lucky inside the time vortex, O Myron," Marsy Batter said. "Do not rely on being lucky twice." She turned to A.L. "You have worked hard to become a P'yugch Person," she said. "Perhaps it is time your wish was granted." She aimed her blaster at his head.

"Marsy," A.L. said. His tentacles curled and uncurled like crazy.

Seeing him so nervous gave Myron a certain amount of pleasure.

"How nice to see you," A.L. went on. "But you didn't have to come. I was going to bring The Myron as soon as my second pumpkin was ripe."

"I'm afraid it's too late for that," Marsy

Batter said. "You have failed me once too often."

A.L. smiled without certainty. Apparently, he had as little idea as the rest of them what Marsy Batter was capable of. Myron felt that he was in the middle of a nightmare. Fear was a sharp taste of metal in his mouth.

"When will you learn, A.L., that I am the master?" Marsy Batter asked with some sorrow. "Give me the ring-flinger."

"You know about that?" A.L. asked.

"My, *ahem*, tentacles are everywhere," she assured him.

Myron hoped that Marsy Batter would not notice that Princess was the one holding the weapon under discussion, but A.L. pointed at her.

"Give me the ring-flinger," Marsy Batter requested. She pointed the blaster at Princess.

Myron had run out of ideas. Any second Marsy Batter would blast Princess to atoms and take the ring-flinger. How could he possibly stop her?

H.G. jumped lightly onto the rim of the

vat and slowly circled the green mush, howl-
ing all the time. She'd chosen a bad moment
to demand dinner, Myron thought.

"That's her," A.L. said. "That's the fur
ball."

"*Was* the fur ball," Marsy Batter said, and
leveled the blaster at H.G.

"No!" Myron and Princess cried.

Marsy Batter fired the blaster, and Myron
was blinded for a second by the flash. When
he could see again the barn was in pieces.
Every plank, board, and splinter floated
slowly outward, trailing a rainbow. Myron's
skin tingled, and something roared like the
sound of wind through an ancient forest. The
explosion seemed to go on for hours.

As suddenly as it had begun the effect
stopped. Bits of the barn that were still in the
air arced over Myron at normal speed and
plopped into the dirt. He sat up and found
that he was covered with sawdust and wood
chips that had stuck to the layer of p'yugch
he'd not yet had a chance to wash off.

Princess was also covered with the remains
of the barn. Behind her was the pumpkin

Marsy Batter had arrived in; it appeared un-harmed but for a thin film of sawdust. A.L. and Marsy Batter were gone, along with H.G. Wells.

"Pretty neat," Princess said thoughtfully. "You add too much energy too fast to dan-delion mush, and *ka-blooie*."

"*Ka-blooie*," Myron agreed. He released an imaginary explosion into the air from his hands. "Did you see where H.G. went?" he asked hopefully.

"Didn't she get away?"

"I don't know." He felt as if he'd lost a best friend. He was amazed at how attached to that cat he'd become in just a couple of days.

"I guess you were right about p'yugch pro-tecting anything it covers from temporal explosions."

"Yeah," Myron said, not as pleased as he wanted to be. Where was H.G.? He picked at the pumpkin unravelings that covered him. He and Princess were covered in p'yugch, and they were still here. A.L. and Marsy Batter had been clean, and they were gone, probably out on the graylands somewhere.

H.G. had been clean, too. Where was she? "I think she's gone," he said.

"Gone?"

"Yeah. She was clean. She went wherever A.L. and Marsy Batter went."

"That's awful."

"Yeah. But I think she knew what she was doing. I think she did it on purpose to save us and to defeat Marsy Batter."

"We may find her yet."

"I don't think so." Myron felt a little better believing that H.G. had voluntarily sacrificed herself rather than just gotten caught in somebody else's battle—but not much. He scraped some p'yugch off his face and flung it down. Accidentally some of it splattered onto Princess. Of course, she was already covered in the stuff.

"Hey," she cried, and gathered a handful of p'yugch from the floor. She heaved it at Myron.

He gathered some up and threw it back at her. Soon they were throwing p'yugch at each other as if it were snow and laughing so hard they could hardly catch their breaths.

After a while they stopped laughing and just sat on the floor, moving the p'yugch around, finger painting with it. Myron was still covered with muck, but he no longer cared. There were worse things than having dirty hands.

"What happened to the ring-flinger?" Myron asked. He looked around.

"Gone with the p'yugch, I guess," Princess said.

She was right, Myron decided. The ring-flinger could be anywhere, including out in the graylands along with A.L., Marsy Batter, and H.G.

"Not a bad performance for a boy accountant," Princess said.

"About average for a boy accountant who also likes comic books." He chuckled happily. It was a real chuckle, not like the kind A.L. used.

"You decided you can do both?"

"Why not? The only thing stopping me is me."

Uncle Hugo walked into what was left of the barn. He was still wearing his suit, of course. "What happened here?" he asked while he glanced around at the destruction and the giant pumpkin with amazement.

"The dandelion mush exploded again," Myron said. "A.L. got caught in the fallout."

"Really?" Hugo said. "What about the big pumpkin?"

"It's kind of a time machine," Myron said.

"You don't say!" Uncle Hugo said as he began to inspect it. "How did it get here?"

"Through time?" Princess suggested.

He knew their explanations could not possibly satisfy Uncle Hugo, but Myron wasn't ready for the questions that Uncle Hugo was bound to ask. First, he wanted a shower, some food, and a nap, in that order. "How did your meeting go?"

"They remember what Birdseye did with frozen food, and they smell profit." Hugo turned to face them. "A.L. is gone, you say?"

"But I'll bet he left his truck," Princess said.

"Well," Hugo said eagerly, "let's take a look at it, then."

"How about a hot shower first?" Myron asked. Princess wanted a shower too.

"I suppose," Hugo said. He seemed to notice for the first time what a mess they were. "You can certainly use one. What have you two been doing?"

Myron sighed. "It turned out that Princess and I were right about A.L. He wanted to take me to the future."

"Aboard this pumpkin?" Hugo asked.

Myron nodded.

"What's wrong with that?"

"It's a long story," Princess told him.

"I guess I can stand not hearing it until you're ready to tell it to me," Uncle Hugo said. He contemplated the big pumpkin.

"Soon," Myron promised.

"I want to take a look at that truck," Uncle Hugo said, "but I'm going to nose around this pumpkin first. Pumpkins decay, trucks don't."

"Too bad you don't have a dandelionboard box big enough to hold it," Princess said.

Myron was surprised. "You told me you thought this business with the dandelions was all fantasyland stuff," he said to her.

"Yeah, well," she said, shrugging. "It *could* work."

"It *could*, yes," Uncle Hugo said as he ran his hand over the smooth surface of the pumpkin. "You two go on back to the house."

Going back to the house was fine with Myron. The last thing he wanted at the moment was another adventure, even if it was only scientific. As a matter of fact, he wasn't sure that he wanted to have the adventure he'd just had. "You know," he said, "if I make sure I don't leave that catalog in the keeper box with my comics, Marsy Batter will never hear about me, and we could avoid—could have avoided—all this trouble."

"Run that by me again," Princess said.

"Marsy Batter knew about me only because of the catalog. If she hadn't seen the catalog, she would not have known my name and she never would have sent A.L. to pick me up."

"Who's Marsy Batter?" Hugo asked.

"Another long story," Myron assured him.

"In any case," said Hugo, "you could do that thing with the catalog, but if you do, the Myron and Princess behind you in the time stream will work at Astronetics for the rest of the summer instead of having the adventure."

Myron studied his uncle Hugo warily. "What do you mean?"

"Well, I could see you really hated working with the dandelions. I thought you'd enjoy working at Astronetics more than helping me. Only A.L.'s arrival prevented me from setting it up. We all got a little busy."

Myron was horrified, and he could see that Princess was too. The last thing either of them wanted was a regular summer job—especially since they both knew that the whole business with A.L. and Marsy Batter turned out so well.

"No," said Myron. "That's all right. I think I'll just leave the catalog where it is."

"Whatever you say," Uncle Hugo said.

"Personally," said Princess, "I'd like to try out that truck. Think of the places we could visit."

Myron could see that Princess was already eager for another adventure. She was a glutton for punishment.

Summoned relentlessly by food, hot water, and soft beds, Myron and Princess walked down the gravel driveway back to the mansion, leaving Uncle Hugo to thump the big pumpkin. The evening was crisp and beautiful, but the fact it had come at all astonished Myron a little. How long had he spent in the graylands? He couldn't remember the last time he'd slept or eaten. Of course, concepts like night and day didn't mean much when you were dealing with time machines.

Myron and Princess casually discussed the nature of time and the opportunities provided by the truck and the two pumpkins they now had at their disposal—the second one A.L. had planted, and the one Marsy Batter arrived in.

Collecting comic books was obviously only the first indication that Myron was becoming more like his uncle Hugo. He smiled. He had evidently contracted a sickness after all, though it was not the one he'd expected.

A thought occurred to him. "What I want to know," he said, "is who started that new batch of dandelion mush—the one that blew H.G. and Marsy Batter and A.L. into the graylands?"

"Not your uncle Hugo?"

"He didn't have time before he left for Astronetics. And I didn't do it either."

"Who's left?" Princess asked.

"The cat."

They walked a few steps in silence.

"But how could a cat . . . ?" Princess said.

They thought about how a cat could.

"I guess H.G. Wells was a good name for that cat after all," Myron said.

Myron hoped that H.G. would show up somewhere between the barn and the house, but she didn't. He hoped she was happy, wherever she was.

"You know what really bothers me about the fact that I'm becoming an adventure junkie?" Myron asked as they walked in the back door.

"No," Princess said. "What really bothers you about the fact that you're becoming an adventure junkie?

"The thing that really bothers me," Myron said, "is that it doesn't bother me."

Princess nodded. "Dibs on the shower," she said.

TIME LEAP V

A CALICO CAT SCAMPERS ACROSS A MONOTONOUS LANDSCAPE OF GRAY GRIT. SHE STOPS OCCASIONALLY TO SNIFF AT THE FOG COVERING A PATCH OF DANDELIONS.

SHE IS SITTING, VIGOROUSLY LAPPING HER TAIL WITH HER TONGUE, WHEN THE GROUND SHAKES AND THE AIR IN FRONT OF HER SHIMMERS. SHE STOPS WASHING.

A MACHINE APPEARS AS IF IT IS CONDENSING OUT OF THE SHIMMERING AIR ITSELF. IT LOOKS LIKE A POLISHED BRASS SLEIGH WITH ADDITIONS AND MODIFICATIONS, AMONG THEM A LARGE BRASS DISK THAT ROTATES RAPIDLY BUT WHICH SLOWS TO A STOP AS THE MAN SITTING IN THE CHAIR BEHIND THE CONTROL PANEL PULLS THE CRYSTAL CONTROL LEVER BACK TO ITS REST POSITION.

THE MAN IS IN HIS MID-TWENTIES. HE SPORTS A LARGE WALRUS MUSTACHE AND WEARS A NEAT TWEED SUIT. THE CAT LOOKS AT HIM SOLEMNLY.

"HERE, WEENA,"
THE MAN CALLS, AND PATS
HIS LAP INVITINGLY.
"HERE, WEENA. GOOD GIRL."

THE CAT LEAPS INTO THE MAN'S
LAP AND PURRS.

AS HE STROKES HER
FROM EARS TO TAIL AND TELLS HER
WHAT A GOOD GIRL SHE IS, HE
LOOKS AROUND WITH
GREAT INTEREST.

AT LAST HE NODS AND PUSHES
FORWARD ON THE CRYSTAL CONTROL
LEVER. THE DISK SPINS FASTER AND
STARTS TO WHINE. AT LAST MACHINE,
MAN, AND CAT GROW INDISTINCT.

WITH A RISING WHISTLE THEY
DISAPPEAR ENTIRELY, LEAVING
BEHIND ONLY AN ORANGE GLOW AND
THE SMELL OF OZONE. SOON, EVEN
THOSE ARE GONE.